LIVING NIGHTMARE

"Fant! Fa...

Dear Spiri... ...n sheer astonishmen... *was it?* Never, not even in his wildest imaginings, would he have envisioned such a deformed monstrosity as now confronted him.

Fant shuffled forward, using its arms and two good legs for support, its third leg dragging on the ground, useless.

The Wacks were all on their feet, moving backward, edging away from the approaching beast.

No! Blade surged against the ropes that bound him, fiercely wrenching his arms and legs, asserting his strength to the utmost, sweat running from every pore. He wasn't going to die like this, helpless, eaten alive!

Also by David Robbins:

THE WERELING
ENDWORLD: THE FOX RUN
ENDWORLD 2: THIEF RIVER FALLS RUN

DAVID ROBBINS

ENDWORLD

TWIN CITIES
RUN

LEISURE BOOKS ✷ NEW YORK CITY

Dedicated to Judy and Joshua:
Double the joy.

A LEISURE BOOK

Published by

Dorchester Publishing Co., Inc.
6 East 39th Street
New York NY 10016

Printed in the United States of America

TWIN CITIES
RUN

OUR STORY SO FAR . . .

It's one hundred years after World War III.

There are survivors.

Before the inevitable came to pass, a wealthy filmmaker named Kurt Carpenter established a survivalist retreat in northwestern Minnesota, near Lake Bronson State Park. Carpenter planned wisely, providing ample provisions for the Home, as he dubbed the site, and detailed instructions for his followers, the ones he called his beloved Family. One of those instructions: to protect themselves, the members of the Family should not attempt to contact the outside world until it became absolutely necessary.

It's necessary.

A form of premature senility is affecting Family members. The current Leader, wise Plato, decides to send one of the Warrior Triads out on a dangerous mission. Using the SEAL, a prototype vehicle Carpenter spent millions developing before the war, the Warriors must travel to the Twin Cities of Minneapolis and St. Paul and attempt to find certain scientific and medical equipment and supplies.

Life after World War III has done a radioactive flip-flop, and between the radiation and the chemical weapons unleashed on the environment, those still alive never know what to expect next. Menace is everywhere. There are the clouds, mysterious green vaporous substances, appearing out of nowhere, devouring all flesh in their path. Hordes of mutates roam the land, deformed former mammals, reptiles, or amphibians, endowed with ravenous appetites, attacking every living thing. Inexplicably, bizarre strains of giantism have developed in select species. New threats arise daily.

Before the Warriors can leave for the Twin Cities, the Home is assaulted by the vicious, plundering Trolls. The conflict between the Family and the Trolls is chronicled in *The Endworld Series #1: The Fox Run.*

A month after the battle with the Trolls, three Warriors and another Family member set out in the SEAL for the Twin Cities. They manage to reach Thief River Falls, where their trip is abruptly curtailed by their confrontation with the enigmatic Watchers and the deadly Brutes. This adventure is related in *The Endworld Series #2: The Thief River Falls Run.* The Family Warriors, and a woman they rescue, a resident of the Twin Cities, are injured in their fight with the Watchers, and they elect to return to the Home to recuperate before attempting to reach the Twin Cities.

Which brings us to: *The Endworld Series #3: The Twin Cities Run . . .*

1

"Did you guys just hear something?"

The four men stopped their activities and listened for a moment.

"I didn't hear a thing," the lean gunman in buckskins replied. His blue eyes twinkled as he grinned at the beautiful, muscular woman standing next to their vehicle. "You must be getting jumpy in your young age!" He placed his hands on the pearl grips to his Colt Pythons, one revolver in a leather holster on each hip, and chuckled. "I knew you'd get antsy," he stated, "the closer we got to Home."

"I ain't jumpy, White Meat!" the woman responded indignantly. "I thought I heard something move in the woods."

"Did you hear anything, Geronimo?" the blond Warrior asked one of his friends.

Geronimo, a superb hunter and tracker, and the only member of the Family with any vestige of Indian blood in his veins, shook his head. "Nope. Sure didn't. But I was talking to Blade." His dark hair swayed as he turned his head, his brown eyes probing the surrounding forest.

David L. Robbins

Blade, the head of the Warrior unit known as Alpha Triad, rose from his kneeling position by the fire he was preparing for their midday meal. His massive muscles rippled in the sunlight, his brawny hands hovering near his prized Bowie knives, as he faced the woman. "Are you positive you heard something, Bertha?" he demanded.

The dusky woman nodded, her curly hair bobbing. "I'm a soldier with the Nomads, remember? I know my business," she affirmed with conviction.

Blade ran his left hand through his wavy dark hair, his gray eyes scanning the nearby trees. It was possible Bertha was mistaken. After all, she had spent her entire life in the Twin Cities, and she was not accustomed to the outdoors and the normal sounds associated with the creatures inhabiting the tall timber.

"I wish we were back at our Home," the fifth and final constituent of their party said, a tall man with flowing brown hair and a beard and moustache.

"We'll be there by tonight, Josh," vowed the gunman. He raised his right hand and felt the stubble on his chin and the corners of his blond handlebar moustache. "Good thing too. I can use a bath and a shave."

"You sure can, Hickok," Geronimo said.

Blade was still trying to detect movement in the nearest undergrowth. Nothing. Bertha must be wrong. He could feel the burning sunlight warming his naked chest, soothing his wounds. The run-in with the Watchers and the Brutes had been costly. He still experienced sharp pain every time he moved, both in the gaping tear in his right shoulder and the bullet crease in his right side.

"You're not exactly a rose either, pard," Hickok commented to Geronimo.

Blade smiled, wondering how Hickok was holding

10

up, knowing the Family's supreme gunfighter was in even worse shape, with a nasty gash over his right eye, and four relatively minor bullet wounds: a nick on his neck, a scrape on his left heel, a furrow along his left side, and a hole in the fleshy part of his left shoulder, almost in the same spot where he had sustained another gunshot during their struggle with the Trolls. If his injuries were bothering him, Hickok was doing a superb job of disguising the fact.

Bertha, the woman they'd saved from the Watchers, had also been hurt. Her left arm was heavily bandaged, the legacy of a Brute's attempt to consume her, to literally eat her alive. Bertha was wearing a baggy flannel shirt, covering the bandage, and jeans confiscated from one of the dead Watchers.

Geronimo, still attired in a green shirt and loose-fitting pants sewn together from the remnants of an old tent, had received several bumps and bruises, but nothing serious.

Of all of them, only the Empath, Joshua, was un-injured. He was standing calmly at the rear of the transport, his hands folded in front of his waist, serenely gazing at some white clouds on the far horizon. Even his clothes, faded brown pants and a light blue shirt made from a discarded sheet, were the least torn and worn. Joshua wore a large Latin cross around his neck.

Blade lazily stretched, relishing the peace and quiet. He had taken a pair of green fatigue pants from one of the larger Watchers, to replace his ragged jeans. Like Hickok, Geronimo, and Joshua, he wore moccasins. Bertha had placed new black boots, again from one of the vanquished Watchers, on her scarred feet, toughened from years of going without shoes. She had giggled when she placed the boots on, delighted at the luxury.

"While you're getting the fire started," Hickok said, addressing Blade, "I reckon I'm going to go water a tree."

"Water a tree?" Bertha repeated, puzzled.

"It's his quaint, if dumb, way of saying he's going to take a piss," Geronimo explained.

"I still can't get used to the way he talks sometimes," Bertha mentioned as Hickok strolled off.

"He thinks he's talking like the real Wild Bill Hickok would," Geronimo said, grinning. "Let's keep it as our little secret that he sounds like a jerk." He winked at Bertha and she laughed.

Hickok had reached the line of trees and he glanced over his shoulder. The SEAL, resembling for all the world the picture of a vehicle called a van he had seen in an automotive book in the enormous Family library, was parked in the center of Highway 59, or what was left of the roadway after a century of neglect and pounding by the elements. If all went as planned, after a quick repast, they would continue north until they hit Highway 11, head east, and be at the Home by dark.

The vegetation at the side of the road was dense. Hickok pushed his way through, searching for a suitable tree. While still a youngster, he had developed a penchant for urinating on the biggest, tallest tree he could find. The habit had become almost a ritual, his way of telling life to get screwed for the bum steer he'd been handed. Why couldn't he have been born before the Big Blast, before everything bit the dust?

Several chickadees were chirping nearby, and two flies buzzed around his head as he approached his intended target.

Why, he wondered, was he suddenly peeing so frequently? Did it have something to do with the constant bouncing around in the SEAL? Maybe he should have the Healers check him over after they returned to Home.

Hickok reached the towering Northern Red oak he'd selected and stared up into the branches high above his head. Had this particular tree been standing before World War III? Would it still be here a hundred years after he passed on to the higher worlds, as Plato referred to them? What would it . . .

The chickadees abruptly ceased their singing, and the entire forest went quiet.

Danger.

Something made a snorting sound, and before the gunman could react, before he could even think about concealing himself, the terror of the woods, the scourge of the land since the Big Blast, ambled around the expansive trunk of the Northern Red oak and stopped four feet away.

Hickok froze.

The creature was a mutate.

No one, not even the wise Family Elders, not even Plato, knew what caused the dreaded mutates. There was speculation the mutates were the result of the combined impact on the environment of the radiation and the chemical weapons unleashed during World War III. But no one really knew, for sure. It was common knowledge the mutates were once reptiles, mammals, or amphibians, transformed into deformed, rampaging killers possessing insatiable appetites. While the animals retained their former size and shape, their entire bodies were covered with large sores, oozing pus everywhere, their skin turning brownish and dehydrated, cracked and peeling. Their ears were mucus-covered stumps, and they breathed in great wheezing gasps. Mutates attacked and consumed any living thing they could catch, and they were utterly fearless. A mutated frog once hopped out of the moat within the Family Home and immediately pounced on the first Family member it saw.

Hickok vividly recalled that incident, and others, and mentally ordered his body to remain immobile. His hands were holding the rawhide tie string to his buckskin pants, and he debated whether he could draw and kill the mutate before it reached him. He enjoyed unquestioned confidence in his speed and ability with his Pythons, but if the mutate didn't die instantly and managed to bite him before it expired, he was as good as dead. Over the years, several Family members had been charged by mutates and survived. Or so they thought. Because if any of the mutate pus managed to enter the human bloodstream, that person died a slow, agonizing death. The pus seemed to cover the area near the mutate's mouths, so any mutate bite was invariably fatal.

What the blazes do I do? Hickok asked himself. Go for his guns and hope he blew the critter away before it sank its gleaming teeth into him? Or wait and see if the mutate noticed him?

This mutate hadn't. Yet. It appeared to have been a fox, probably a red fox, before the mysterious transformation. With its ears covered by the reeking pus, its hearing was diminished, leaving its nose as its primary organ for detection and identification. The mutate's eyesight was unimpaired but, like many animals, it relied on motion to pinpoint other creatures.

I may be in luck here, Hickok speculated. The air was deathly still and would not carry his scent to the mutate. The former fox was not looking at him, but was warily eyeing a leafy bush in the opposite direction. If he didn't move, the mutate might actually walk away.

Instead, the bestial demon turned and looked directly at him.

Hickok involuntarily tensed. He could see the beady brown eyes studying him, the tiny nostrils quivering, as the mutate strove to register this new presence. Maybe the thing would decide he was another tree and leave. He watched the mutate's eyes, anticipating a reaction.

He got it.

The mutate's eyes suddenly widened, the fox snarled, and it came at him, leaping.

His hands a blur, Hickok drew the Colts, using his thumbs to pull back the hammers as he leveled the Pythons, his fingers pulling their respective triggers as the mutate reached the apex of its jump. The blast of the .357 Magnums shattered the forest, the slugs catching the mutate in the face and causing it to tumble to the ground at Hickok's feet.

The demented beast snapped at his moccasins.

Hickok stepped back, already cocking the Pythons again.

The mutate thrashed and rose to its feet, wobbly, growling and hissing. It prepared for another spring.

The Colts bucked as Hickok fired each gun twice more, the bullets slamming the mutate to the turf.

The fox twitched briefly, wheezed, and expired.

Close, brother! Too close! Hickok leaned against the tree and sighed, relieved.

"Over here!" someone shouted. Sounded like Joshua.

"No!" another person yelled, and this time Hickok definitely indentified Geronimo's voice. "It came from over here!"

There was a crashing in the underbrush, and

Blade, Geronimo, Joshua, and Bertha broke from cover and abruptly stopped at the sight of Hickok and the dead mutate.

"Lordy!" Bertha exclaimed, grimacing. "An Ugly!" The residents of the Twin Cities referred to the mutates as Uglies. Her vocabulary was peppered with street slang and what Joshua called "cute colloquialism." She was carrying a Smith and Wesson Model 3000 Pump shotgun taken from a Watcher Geronimo had killed.

"Thank the Spirit you're not injured!" Joshua stated, his right hand holding a Ruger Redhawk .44 Magnum.

Blade was frowning at the body of the mutate, cradling his Commando Arms Carbine in his arms. He hated the mutates; one of them had been responsible for slaying his father. In addition to the Commando and his Bowie knives, Blade carried two Solingen throwing knives in a leather sheath fastened to his belt, secured in the small of his broad back. Never satisfied with just a few blades, he also had a folding Buck knife in his right front pocket as well as a dagger strapped to his right calf and another to his left wrist. Fortunately, he had been able to retrieve most of his weapons after the battle in Thief River Falls.

"What happened?" Geronimo asked Hickok. "Did you take a leak on it?" He was armed with a Browning B-80 Automatic Shotgun, an Arminius .357 in a shoulder holster under his right arm, and two genuine Apache tomahawks tucked under his belt.

Hickok grinned. "Not quite, pard," he replied. "We argued over which of us was going to use the tree first, and he lost."

"Did it bite you?" Blade inquired, concerned.

"Nope," Hickok answered.

"Are you positive?" Blade pressed him.

"Don't you think I'd know if it did?" Hickok retorted.

"I don't see why we're worried," Geronimo noted.

"What do you mean?" Joshua asked.

"If the mutate bit Hickok," Geronimo cracked, "the poor mutate would be the one to kick the bucket."

"Very funny," Hickok rejoined.

"Where's your Henry?" Blade wanted to know, alluding to Hickok's rifle, a Navy Arms Henry.

"Left it in the SEAL," Hickok admitted sheepishly.

"Next time," Blade advised him, "don't go into the woods without it."

Hickok twirled the Pythons and slid the Colts into their holsters. "These babies took care of it. I didn't need the Henry."

"What if it had been something larger?" Blade demanded.

"I can handle myself, pard." Hickok smiled. "You know that."

"I know." Blade nodded. "I also know you're overconfident, and one day that character flaw will get you into trouble."

"Why don't you head back to the SEAL?" Hickok said, changing the subject.

"Aren't you coming?" Bertha asked.

"I've got something to do," Hickok told her.

"Like what?" she questioned.

Hickok grabbed the tie string. "Three guesses."

"Oh." Bertha turned away.

"What about you guys?" Hickok glanced at Geronimo, Joshua, and Blade. "You planning to stay and watch?"

"No, thanks," Geronimo declined. "We left our

magnifying glass at the Home."

Blade and Bertha laughed, and all four of them strolled off, heading for the transport.

Hickok rolled his blue eyes skyward. "Comedians!" he muttered. "The world is full of comedians!"

2

"Wow!" Bertha declared excitedly. "I just can't believe I'm really here!"

Blade had braked the SEAL at the edge of the cleared field bordering the western wall of the Home, the wall containing the only means of entering and exiting the compound, a drawbridge.

"You better believe it, Black Beauty," Hickok assured her. "This is our Home."

Blade was driving, Geronimo sitting in the other bucket seat in the front of the SEAL. Hickok, Bertha, and Joshua were seated in the back seat. A large space in the rear of the vehicle was devoted to storing their provisions. At the moment, it was filled to the roof with the items they had confiscated from the Watchers in Thief River Falls.

"The Home is so big!" Bertha marveled. "It's even bigger than I imagined it would be."

"Our Home embraces thirty acres," Joshua explained to her. "It's completely enclosed within a twenty-foot-high brick wall. We keep the area outside the walls, about one hundred and fifty yards all around the Home, free of trees and brush and

19

boulders, anything an enemy could utilize in an assault. Notice the top of the wall." Joshua pointed with his right hand. "That's barbed wire." He sighed. "We certainly exemplify the concept of spiritual love, don't we?"

"Give me a break, Josh!" Hickok responded. "If the Home wasn't as well protected as it is, the Family wouldn't have survived this long after the Big Blast."

"I suppose you're correct," Joshua reluctantly agreed. "Anyway," he continued, "we receive our water from a stream. It enters the property under the northwest corner of the wall, and flows out under the southeastern corner. By digging a trench along the inner base of the wall, the Family has constructed a moat, another line of defense in case of an attack."

"What's it like inside?" Bertha inquired as Blade drove toward the drawbridge, which was closed.

"The eastern half is devoted to agriculture and preserved in a natural state," Joshua elaborated. "In the center are the cabins for the married couples, and the western section has our six main buildings, six concrete blocks arranged in a triangular fashion. You'll see them in a moment."

The drawbridge was being lowered as they approached.

"You dummies can't know what a place like this means," Bertha said in a low voice. "A place where a person can be safe, where no one is trying to kill you. It's incredible!"

"After the experiences we had in Fox and Thief River Falls," Blade stated over his right shoulder, "I think we have some idea of what you're talking about."

"It's really that bad in the Twin Cities?" Hickok asked Bertha.

She looked at him and nodded. "You have no idea, White Meat. You have no idea."

The drawbridge was fully extended, and Blade turned onto it and wheeled the SEAL into the Home.

"Look at all of them!" Bertha cried out.

The Family was gathered for their homecoming, having been appraised of their return by one of the Warrior guards on the wall.

Blade smiled when he spotted Jenny, his intended, and Plato, the Family Leader, standing side by side. Next to Plato stood his wife, Nadine.

"Lordy! They're all starin' at us!" Bertha slid closer to Hickok. "There must be sixty or seventy of them!"

The gunman chuckled. "Don't worry, gorgeous. They won't bite you!"

Blade stopped the green transport, the mammoth tires flinging dirt and dust into the air at his abrupt braking. He flung his door open and jumped down.

"Blade!" Jenny yelled, and then she was in his arms.

Blade embraced her, emotionally overwhelmed by his affection. He had come so close to buying the farm in Thief River Falls, and now he was holding her, touching her, and delighting in the sight of her blonde hair and blue eyes.

It all seemed too good to be true!

"You're back!" Jenny declared. She squeezed him and felt him flinch. "What's wrong?" she asked, stepping back, searching his face. "You've been hurt!"

"Just a few scatches," Blade told her. "It's no big deal."

Plato, his long gray hair and beard whipping in the gusty breeze, approached and took Blade's right hand. "It is good to see you, but we didn't expect you back so soon."

"He's been hurt," Jenny said, her lovely face reflecting her anxiety.

"Actually," Blade corrected her, "we're all pretty beat up. Hickok and Bertha should see the Healers right away."

"That's why you've returned?" Plato inquired.

"Sorry," Blade said. "I know you wanted us to get to the Twin Cities as fast as we could. We reached Thief River Falls and all hell broke loose."

Plato's stooped, frail frame turned toward C Block, the Family infirmary. "You can provide the essential details after the Healers have examined you. You . . ." He paused, eyeing Blade quizzically. "Did you say Bertha?"

Blade grinned and pointed.

"Well, I'll be . . ." Plato began, at a loss for words.

"It's a black woman!" Jenny exclaimed.

"Half and half," Blade amended. "One of her parents was white."

The Family was clustered about the SEAL, many trying to peer in the windows for a glimpse of Bertha. The SEAL's bulletproof plastic body was tinted to prevent anyone outside from viewing the interior, but several members of the Family were able to see Bertha through the open door Blade had exited from.

Inside the transport, Bertha was clinging to Hickok. "Why are they all lookin' at me like that? Tell them to cut it out!"

Hickok was grinning. "You can't blame them. You're the first black woman they've ever seen, and you're pretty to boot."

"I don't like people staring at me," Bertha snapped.

"The Family had a black couple in the early days after the war," Geronimo informed her. He was still sitting in the front seat. Joshua was already outside, embracing his parents, Solomon and Ruth. "Unfortunately, they perished before they could bear any children," Geronimo continued. "Kurt Carpenter, the man responsible for constructing the Home and picking the couples who joined him here right before the Big Blast, left a diary. In it, he says he tried to select people of different ethnic backgrounds. My own parents were Indian. They passed on when I was younger."

"Is that man Chinese?" Bertha asked, indicating a small, wiry man carrying a long, black scabbard. "And what's that he's got in his hands?"

Geronimo smiled. "That's Rikki-Tikki-Tavi, and the thing he's holding is his katana. He's a Warrior, like us. And, yes, he does have some Chinese blood. He's the head of Beta Triad."

"You mean," Bertha asked in clarification, "like Blade is the head of you guys, of the Alpha Triad?"

Geronimo nodded. "The Family has four Warrior Triads, and we're hoping to add another soon. Blade not only heads Alpha Triad, he's also in charge of all the Warriors."

"I sure do wish they'd stop staring," Bertha nervously reiterated.

"Well, we can't sit in here all night," Hickok stated as he reached for the door, extending his right hand.

"No!" Bertha clutched Hickok's arm. "Give me time to . . ." Her hands closed on a hard object, apparently fastened to Hickok's right wrist, hidden under the sleeve of his buckskins. "What's this thing?" she asked, beginning to pull the sleeve up.

Hickok extracted his arm from her grip, grinning. "It's a Mitchell's Derringer, a two-shot .38. One of my backup guns. I also have a four shot C.O.P., in .357 caliber, strapped to my left calf."

"I didn't know that," Bertha said.

"We learn something new every day," Hickok philosophized.

"Smart butt!" Bertha retorted.

"Quit stallling, Black Beauty," Hickok directed. "Open the door. The sun is almost below the horizon. We're losing the light."

"I don't know . . ." Bertha hedged.

"Never took you for a wimp," Hickok joked, and quickly opened the door before she could stop him.

The Family members backed away, respectfully providing room near the door.

Bertha took a deep breath. "Here goes nothin'!"

"Would you rather be back in the Twin Cities?" Hickok inquired.

Bertha vigorously shook her head. "You got a point." She climbed from the transport and faced the crowd with a wide smile. "Hi, there, people!" she greeted them. "You're probably wondering why I called you all together!"

No one laughed.

Hickok jumped down and stood at Bertha's side.

"I'm in big trouble here," Bertha whispered confidentially.

Plato moved through the throng and reached the gunman and his newfound friend. "Salutations, sister." He offered his hand in friendship. "My cognomen is Plato. On behalf of my brethren, I cordially welcome you to our humble abode."

Bertha took his hand and limply shook it, her eyes widening as she glanced repeatedly from Hickok to the old man. Finally, she released her hold and placed her mouth against Hickok's left ear. "What did that bozo just say?"

Hickok, chuckling, put his lips near her right ear. "This bozo is Plato, our Family Leader. He just said hello. I should warn you, he likes to use a lot of fancy words."

"I'm in big trouble here," Bertha quietly repeated. She turned to Plato, beaming. "I'm happy to meet you, gramps."

Hickok snickered.

"Did I say something wrong?" Bertha nervously asked.

"Nonsense, my girl," Plato said reassuringly. "Nathan is simply displaying his warped sense of humor."

"Who's Nathan?" Bertha wanted to know.

Plato indicated Hickok.

Bertha seemed perplexed. "Nathan? I thought his name was Hickok. That's what they told me it was."

"Nathan is how he was known before his Naming," Plato explained, carefully selecting his words. He'd overheard Bertha's remarks concerning his vocabulary. "All of us have the option, the choice, of picking our own names when we turn sixteen. Our founder, Kurt Carpenter, initiated, began the practice. You see, Carpenter was worried we'd forget about what it was like before the Third World War. He thought we should stay in touch with our roots by searching the history books in our library and choosing any name we wanted as our own. It's not mandatory, simply encouraged. The practice cultivates a distinct appreciation of our cultural and historical antecedents," Plato concluded, forgetting himself.

"Say what?" Bertha responded, confused.

"It helps us remember who we are and how we got here," Plato explained.

"I got here in this buggy of yours," Bertha said, her left thumb jerking toward the SEAL.

"You are welcome," Plato stated earnestly.

David L. Robbins

"You'll let me stay, won't you?" Bertha asked apprehensively. "I give you my word I'll behave myself. I won't get drunk, and I won't start fights unless someone else starts one first, and I'll do any work you want, and I won't spit on your grass 'cause I know some people get finnicky over spitting, and I'll kill anyone you want me to, because I'm real good at . . ."

Plato held up his right hand, cutting her off. "Slow down, child! You're among friends. We have one law here, one rule you must follow. Whatever else you do is up to you, within reasonable limits, of course."

"Of course," Bertha agreed. She pondered a moment. "What's this rule you have?"

"Love."

"Come again?"

"You must try to love your brothers and your sisters, even as you think they should love you," Plato said, stating the Family's cardinal mandate.

"Wow!" was all Bertha could think to say.

"After you have eaten and rested, come see me," Plato directed. "We'll talk."

Bertha nodded, happily watching as the Family Leader walked off.

"Well," Hickok prodded her, "what do you think of the Home now that you're here?"

Bertha contentedly gazed at the dozens of friendly, open faces staring at her. She sighed and clasped her arms across her chest, slowly swaying.

"I think I'm in heaven!"

3

In the quiet hours of early morning, an hour before sunrise, a figure dressed in black, including a mask to conceal his face, hastily crossed the field west of the Home and reached the wall undetected. He took several seconds to listen, gripping the rope and the steel hook in his right hand. A black holster hung on his left hip, containing a special automatic pistol of indeterminate origin. Fastened to his belt above his right hip was a black pouch, filled with the essential items required for his nocturnal mission: the plastic explosive, the detonator, and the timer.

The saboteur knew a guard, one of the Warriors, patrolled the wall above his head, but the Warrior on duty was well north of his position and wouldn't return for a minimum of five minutes, allowing ample opportunity for him to scale the wall.

Moving swiftly, expertly, the man swung the steel hook in an ever-enlarging circle. At the proper instant, maintaining optimum speed and calculating the precise angle, he flung the grappling hook upward and was rewarded for his effort when the hook caught in the barbed wire on top of the wall.

The man in black hurriedly climbed the rope, effortlessly hauling his powerful frame to the lip of the brick wall. He paused to ascertain the Warrior's location, then deftly parted the barbed wire and crawled under the sharp barbs.

The compound below was deserted.

The saboteur was lying on the wall, only ten feet north of the drawbridge. On each side of the closed drawbridge, crossing over the flowing moat, supported by sturdy beams, wooden steps led from the wall to the ground. The commando ran down the nearest stairs and dropped flat, listening to determine if he'd been detected.

The Family Home was silent, except for the chirping of the crickets and the singing of the birds.

The figure in black knew the layout of the Home by rote. The six concrete blocks were spaced one hundred yards apart, forming a perfect triangle, with A Block, as the Family called the southern-most structure, forming one point. Next came B Block, one hundred yards to the northwest. Third, C Block, was another one hundred yards northwest of B Block, and the western tip of the triangle, situated the closest to the drawbridge. D Block was a hundred yards east of C Block, followed by E Block on the eastern point. One hundred yards southwest of E Block was F Block, and the triangle was completed by A Block. The commando also knew the purpose of each of the Blocks. A Block was the armory, B the sleeping quarters for unmarried Family members, C Block, the infirmary, D Block was the construction area and carpentry shop, E was the library, and F Block was used for storing argricultural supplies and preserving and preparing the Family food.

The saboteur darted across the compound and safely reached the corner of C Block. He entertained

28

the notion of using his explosive on the Blocks, but disregarded the idea. His superiors were quite specific in their orders, and he dared not disobey. Not if he valued his life. No, the Blocks weren't his target. He was after the SEAL. Cautiously, he peeked around the corner and spotted the vehicle parked in the center of the cleared area between the Blocks. It was exactly where the infrared had revealed it would be.

Smiling under his mask, the commando jogged toward the transport, keeping his body low, minimizing his profile. This assignment was proceeding smoothly. He'd be able to achieve his objective and depart before these dimwits knew what hit them!

Someone coughed, and the dark figure dropped and flattened. He could see a Family member coming from the direction of D Block, heading his way. What the hell was someone doing up so early? He held his breath and tensed, hoping the fool would bypass him.

The early bird continued walking directly toward him.

He could not afford to waste precious time. Slowly, he eased the pistol from its holster and sighted on the approaching person, a man. When the unsuspecting victim was fifteen yards distant, he squeezed the trigger and watched as the heavy slug ripped through the man's chest and knocked him to the turf. The silenced pistol produced a slight whishing noise.

Satisfied with his shot and positive the Family member was dead, the commando holstered the pistol and stood. Timing for this venture was critical. He'd been instructed to insure the explosion occurred an hour after sunrise, when the area would be packed with the members of the Family. They invariably congregated here after first light to engage in their morning worship.

The saboteur casually walked to the SEAL, forcing his nerves to remain calm. No one would realize he wasn't a Family member until they were right on top of him, and he wasn't about to let any of them get that close.

The Warrior on the west wall was gazing at the field and the forest beyond, unaware an intruder was in the compound.

Grinning, the commando reached the vehicle and crouched next to the front tire on the driver's side. The tires were huge, the body of the SEAL resting several feet off the ground. He reached into his pouch and removed the packet of plastic explosive.

"Are you the new chauffeur?" a deep voice behind him asked.

Instinctively, the saboteur dropped the packet and whirled, going for his automatic. He recognized the wavy hair and massive muscles belonging to the one they called Blade, their chief Warrior, and he marveled at the stealth displayed, the skill necessary to sneak up on him, even as he drew the pistol.

Blade lunged, grabbing the man in black by the wrists and hauling him to his feet. His shoulders and arms rippling, Blade twisted his opponent's left wrist. "Drop it, or I'll snap your wrists!" he barked.

In response, the commando slammed his right knee into Blade's groin area.

Blade grunted, then savagely wrenched on the left wrist he held, bending it back. The pistol fell to the grass, and Blade forcefully smashed his foe into the SEAL. "I want some answers from you, and I want them now!"

The commando was an expert at his craft. He swept his forehead back and up, driving it against

Blade's chin, momentarily stunning the Warrior and causing him to relax his grasp. The saboteur moved swiftly, putting his left foot behind Blade's ankles and heaving, knocking the Warrior to the ground. He wrenched his hands free from Blade's clutches and dove for his pistol.

Blade rolled to his feet, drawing his right Bowie and throwing, the keen blade imbedding itself in the commando's left shoulder as he picked up the pistol. The man in black spun and fell onto his back, still clinging to the automatic. Before Blade could reach him, he tossed the pistol from his left hand to his right, flicking a small lever above the trigger from SINGLE to FULL AUTO.

His body moving with incredible speed for one so large, Blade dove under the transport, seeking the protection of the SEAL's bulletproof body.

The commando fired as he rose to his knees, the bullets striking the vehicle and ricocheting off, the slugs missing Blade by a fraction as he disappeared from view. Leaning over, the saboteur peered under the transport, his pistol at the ready. There was no sign of the red-headed Warrior. Stymied, the man in black rose, resisting the excruciating pain in his injured shoulder, and alertly moved around the SEAL, surmising Blade was hiding behind one of the large tires.

The Warrior was gone.

The saboteur calmly scanned the area, puzzled. The closest cover, a stand of trees, was at least twenty-five yards away. Blade couldn't possibly have reached those trees. But where could he be? The commando knew he must eliminate the Warrior before departing the Home. Leaving no witnesses was a prime directive. His shoulder was throbbing, but he ignored the agony, sweat beading his brow under the wool mask. An operative of his expertise was thoroughly trained, including intensive courses on the conscious suppression of pain. The mission came first; nothing else mattered.

The Warrior must be circling the vehicle.

Treading softly, the commando eased around the rear of the SEAL, his automatic ready.

Again, no one.

Stumped, the figure in black crouched and looked under the transport one more time. Where the hell was Blade? As he slowly straightened, the saboteur saw the ladder leading to the roof of the SEAL. At his briefing—was it just ten hours ago?—he was told the Family vehicle was solar powered, so the metal rungs must permit anyone to climb to the roof and inspect the collectors. . . .

The roof!

Sensing he was too late, the commando spun, aiming his pistol upward.

The Warrior was perched at the edge of the roof, his other Bowie already in his hand. He swept his arm down, and the heavy knife flew, slicing into the saboteur's throat and ripping through his jugular.

Gasping, the commando dropped the pistol and stumbled to his knees. In vain, he attempted to pull the Bowie from his neck. Blood was flowing over his chest, thick, rich streams of red.

Blade jumped from the top of the SEAL, landing lightly beside his foe.

Gurgling, the man in black looked up at Blade, his eyes pleading for aid.

"There's nothing I can do," Blade informed him.

The saboteur sobbed, his eyes beginning to glaze.

"You shouldn't have shot one of my Family," Blade stated grimly. "I just spotted him from the roof. No one harms one of our Family and gets away with it!"

The man in black was past hearing. He toppled to

the grass, the only sound the peculiar squishing noise his throat made as the blood continued to flow.

Blade turned and ran to the fallen Family member. The sun was beginning to make its presence known. Although the fiery orb was still below the horizon, the sky was becoming lighter.

Who was it?

Blade reached the man and stopped, sadness filling his heart. His assumption proved correct; poor Brian was shot in the heart. Brian was charged with keeping the drawbridge in flawless operating condition. Last evening, while enjoying conversation around a fire, he'd mentioned he was going to rise early and perform some work on the massive mechanism required for raising and lowering the drawbridge. His wife would be devastated.

Why?

Blade clenched his ponderous fists and glared at the rising sun. His sinewy body, fully recuperated after six weeks of rest and rehabilitation, assumed a posture of defiance, his square chin jutting outward. The late August air was cool and refreshing.

Why, Oh Spirit, was it necessary for Brian to die? Why was constant hardship and struggle the lot of those still toiling to wring a living from the hostile land? Maybe Hickok was right. A person should take what they could get while the getting was good. Look at Joshua. He was continually striving to live spiritually, and his inner turmoil never ceased. The run to Thief River Falls had been a horrifying experience for Joshua, yet Hickok had enjoyed himself immensely. Hickok craved action, Joshua longed for peace. They were living, sterling examples of diametrically opposed viewpoints. Which one of them was right? Hickok? Or Joshua? The preeminent gunfighter or the spirit child of a Cosmic Creator? Or was the answer lying somewhere between the two extremes, somewhere . . . .

Footsteps sounded behind him.

Blade whirled, mentally lambasting himself for leaving his Bowies in the corpse. The Commando and the Vegas were in B Block, but he still carried the Solingens, the daggers, and his Buck knife. His right hand gripped one of the throwing knives as he turned, expecting another attacker.

It was Plato.

"Commendable reflexes," Plato remarked. "I saw the body near the SEAL. . . ." He stopped, his eyes resting on the form in the grass beside Blade. "Who . . ." he began, then he recognized Brian.

"It's Brian," Blade stated needlessly.

"Oh, dear Lord, no!" Plato said quietly, the wrinkles on his face etched in an expression of profound sorrow. "Not Brian!"

"Afraid so." Blade placed his left arm around Plato's narrow shoulders.

"How did it happen?" Plato asked.

"I didn't see it," Blade replied, "but I surmise the guy in black did it. Brian was probably on his way to the shop. He said he wanted to get an early start on some work on the drawbridge, and you know how conscientious he was."

"I know," Plato affirmed sadly.

"It will be a while before the Family is all up and about," Blade mentioned. "I better remove the body. No need for any of the children to be exposed to this."

"We have some time first," Plato said. "I need to talk with you."

Blade nodded. "I have some things I want to say to you too, but you go first."

"Any idea why the man in black was here?" Plato questioned.

"Not yet," Blade admitted. "Let's check."

They walked to the body of the interloper and Blade knelt, searching the man's pockets and his pouch.

"Anything?" Plato inquired.

"Nope." Blade shook his head. "No identification of any sort. Just his pistol and these two devices in his pouch. One looks like a timing device of some kind. Don't know what the other thing is."

"What does he look like?" Plato asked, pointing at the mask.

Blade pulled the woolen mask over the dead man's face. The stranger had been young, maybe thirty, with brown hair cropped close to his head and a scar on his left cheek.

"Reminds me of a military-style haircut," Plato remarked.

Blade stood and stepped back. He spotted something lying near a front tire, crossed to it, and read the label as he picked it up. "Explosive," he read aloud. "Issue number two-three-seven-seven."

Plato took the packet and studied it. "Thank the Spirit you were able to prevent him from completing his task. We would be lost without the SEAL."

"Thank yourself," Blade corrected as Plato pocketed the packet.

"What do you mean?" his mentor inquired.

"You were the one who told me last night we were to leave today. I was here so early because I was too antsy to sleep. I decided to activate the solar panels so we would have a full charge in those unique batteries Carpenter spent a fortune developing." Using his key, he unlocked the front door and threw a red lever located under the center of the dashboard.

Plato's brow was furrowed as he contemplated the implications. Finally, he glanced at Blade. "I still

want Alpha Triad and Joshua to depart this afternoon for the Twin Cities."

"Are you nuts?" Blade countered.

Plato smiled. "Thoroughly sane, thank you very
much."

"You know what I mean," Blade said, annoyed.
"Think about the potential for harm to the Family
with one of the Warrior Triads out on another run.
Before we left the last time, you said there was a
power-monger in the Family, an aspiring dictator,
someone who wants to forcibly remove you from
your position as our Leader. Then there are the
Watchers. We know very little about them, except
they're deadly and engaged in some sort of contain-
ment strategy. They don't seem to want anyone
running loose over the countryside. Add these
factors up and you'll have to agree we should remain
here."

"I do not agree," Plato replied.

"You are nuts!" Blade snapped.

"Bear with me a moment," Plato patiently
advised. "Granted, you voice serious concerns. I
still refuse to reveal the identity of the power-
monger, but if it will make you any happier, I
promise I will give you his name after you return
from the Twin Cities. I still feel he isn't a grave
threat at this time, and you'll simply need to trust
my judgment."

"What about the Watchers?" Blade quickly interjected.

"They haven't bothered us in the past, so why
should they start now?"

"This guy could be a Watcher, for all we know!"
Blade countered, irritated by Plato's complacency.

"True," Plato acknowledged. "But if the
Watchers are after our transport, and you take the

SEAL with you, we won't pose a threat to them until you return."

"Sheer speculation!" Blade rejoined.

"Granted." Plato sighed and leaned against the SEAL, easing the strain on his arthritic legs. "Until we acquire sufficient data, speculation is all we have. You know how deeply I love you, and I feel you reciprocate. If so, you must trust me in this matter. I firmly believe our beloved Family will be safe while you make a trip to the Twin Cities. Don't tarry. Locate the equipment and supplies the Family needs and get back here as expeditiously as feasible."

"I don't know. . . ." Blade hedged, unwilling to agree.

"Why do I have a distinct feeling of deja vu?" Plato asked.

"I wasn't eager to leave last time," Blade conceded. "I don't like the idea of leaving now any better. In fact, I like it less."

"We'll still have three Warrior Triads guarding the Home," Plato reminded Blade.

"Have the Elders picked any candidates for the new Triad we want to add?" Blade inquired.

"We've selected two of the applicants," Plato answered, "but we have yet to decide on the third. We'll announce them as soon as we do."

Blade faced east, watching the rising sun. "I better get this body out of here."

"You can place it in C Block," Plato suggested.

Blade stooped, lifted the saboteur from the ground, and placed the black-garbed figure over his left shoulder. He casually strolled toward the infirmary.

Plato opted to tag along. "You certainly appear recovered from your injuries," he observed.

Blade whacked his chest with his right palm. "Never better."

"Hickok is also healed?" Plato asked.

"Far as I know," Blade stated. "He was fine yesterday when I saw him playing tag with Star, the Indian girl he rescued before we left for the Twin Cities the last time."

"I've noticed," Plato mentioned, "that Geronimo has been spending a considerable amount of time with Star's mother, Rainbow."

Blade grinned. "I think the whole Family has noticed."

They walked in a northwesterly direction toward C Block. Some members of the Family were up, but none close enough to perceive Blade was toting a body.

"I'd best hurry," Blade said. "I still have to get Brian." He ran ahead of Plato.

The Family Leader stopped and waited, watching as Blade entered the infirmary and exited a moment later without the corpse. Plato dreaded the prospect of informing Brian's mate, Catherine, about his death and announcing it to the Family. Some aspects of leadership were utterly distasteful.

"Let's get Brian," Blade announced as he approached.

"I've been meaning to ask you a question," Plato quickly asked as they hastened to Brian's body.

"What is it?"

"Have you observed any . . ." Plato hesitated, searching for the right word.

"Any what?" Blade urged him.

"Any peculiar behavior on Nathan's part?" Plato finished.

"Peculiar?" Blade repeated.

"Yes. Abnormal. Unusual. Out of character," Plato elaborated.

"None to speak of," Blade stated as he reached Brian and hefted him onto his shoulder. "Why?" They headed for C Block.

"Don't you think he recovered a bit too fast from Joan's demise?" Plato questioned.

Blade considered the query. Joan, a Warrior, had been killed by the Trolls. According to the gossip, Hickok and Joan had been very much in love, both for the first time. "I was there, remember?" Blade said to Plato. "I saw how her death tore him apart."

"At first," Plato agreed. "Oh sure, he moped for a while, about a month. He was severely depressed up to the time he saved Rainbow and Star. Don't you recall?"

"Now that you mention it," Blade admitted, "I do. Right after that incident, he became surprisingly cheerful. And on the ride to Thief River Falls he was downright happy. Odd. I never paid any attention to it until just now."

"You had weightier matters to handle," Plato said. "I probably wouldn't have noticed either. It was Joshua who brought it to my attention."

"Joshua?"

"Yes. He is an Empath, after all. Our youngest and most inexperienced, to be certain, but still talented. Joshua told me he believes Hickok's soul is in danger," Plato intoned gravely.

"I'll keep my eye on him," Blade promised.

"Please do."

They reached C Block and stopped.

"I must go see Catherine," Plato stated, frowning. "Will you insure adequate provisions are loaded into the transport for your departure this afternoon?"

"No problem."

"And tell Hickok, Geronimo, and Joshua so they may bid adieu to their loved ones beforehand,"

Plato added, walking off.

"I will," Blade promised. He entered the infirmary and gently positioned Brian's limp form on one of the dozen cots, next to the one containing the intruder.

Another run. Blade thought of his darling Jenny and grimaced. Twice he'd ventured from the Home in the SEAL, and each time he'd left the safety and security afforded by the encircling brick walls he'd nearly lost his life. Would it happen again? Would his luck fail him this time around? He was finding it harder and harder to leave Jenny. Maybe he should tell Plato to send one of the other Warriors. Rikki-Tikki-Tavi would be the logical choice. Rikki was a supremely skilled fighter, and he was well liked by both Hickok and Geronimo.

Blade moved to the doorway and peered out at the budding day. Jenny would be overjoyed if he remained, but how would the other Family members react? Would they speculate he was losing his nerve? Would they question his ability to lead the Warriors and, perhaps one day, lead the entire Family as Plato intended him to do? More to the point, how would Hickok and Geronimo take the news? They were more than his best friends, companions since childhood; the three of them together were a highly trained unit devoted to the protection of the Home and the preservation of the Family. Everyone knew of the creeping senility affecting the older Family members. How could the future of the Family be assured, the Family itself be preserved, when they were confronted by the bleak prospect of eventual extinction within several generations?

Blade sighed.

No. He had to go. All of his training, all of his

instincts, and the pricking of his conscience prodded him to go.

"I need an edge, though," he said aloud.

And he had one.

Plato expected Alpha Triad and Joshua to make this run to the Twin Cities. Well, one other person was going to make the trip.

Whether she wanted to or not.

4

He located her shortly after the midday meal, seated under a tree all by herself, on the inner bank of the moat. Her back was against the trunk of the maple. The water slowly flowed past her position at the northern edge of the Home, due north of D Block.

"I've been expecting you, Blade," she greeted him as he approached.

"Really? Mind if I join you?" Blade knew she had missed the noon meal and wondered why.

"No," she replied.

Her response caught him off guard. He hesitated in the act of sitting. "No, Bertha?"

She brushed at a fly on her yellow, short-sleeved blouse. Her top complimented her green pants nicely. Someone had given her a pair of moccasins. "Oh, you can sit down." She grinned.

Blade obliged, studying her.

"When I said no," she explained, "I meant the other."

"What other?" he asked.

Bertha deliberately stared into his gray eyes.

42

"Did I do something to stir you up?"

"No. Why?"

"I can't understand why you're insultin' me," she said.

"I'm not insulting you," Blade objected.

"Yes, you are," she countered. "I'm not as stupid as I look."

"I never said you were."

"But you must think I'm stupid," Bertha said harshly, "if you think I don't know why you're here."

"You know?" Blade fidgeted. This wasn't going as he wanted. He needed to regain the initiative.

"Of course. And the answer is no." Bertha turned away and watched a leaf float past.

"You haven't heard what I want to say," Blade commented.

Bertha glared at him. "Who you kiddin'? It will be the same bullshit you fed me in Thief River Falls. I fell for it that time, but not now. I can't seem to get through that thick head of yours."

"Get what through?"

"THAT I DON'T WANT TO GO BACK TO THE TWINS!" Bertha shouted.

Blade, nonplused by her outburst, averted his gaze and played with the grass near his right leg.

"You just don't know, Blade," Bertha said sadly. "You just don't know how bad it is in the Twins. Like I told you before, the place is a madhouse. It isn't bad enough we've got wild animals all over the place, and rats everywhere you turn, but you've also got all the different groups fightin' for control of their measly turf. I'm a Nomad, and we hold most of the north part of the Twins. The Porns control the west, the Horns mostly the east, and the Wacks..." Bertha paused and shuddered. "The Wacks have their base in the south. You never know from one day to the next whether you will still be alive and kickin' that night."

"I can appreciate your position," Blade sympathized.

"You can't appreciate shit," Bertha angrily retorted.

"Can I ask you one question?" Blade asked, ignoring her barb.

"I don't see as how I can stop you, Muscle Head!" Bertha shot back.

"Do you think Hickok, Geronimo, Joshua, and I will be able to locate the items Plato wants with a minimum of difficulty?" Blade queried.

Bertha shook her head. "You ain't ever been to the Twins . . ." she began.

"We've got a map," Blade interrupted.

"Map, schmap!" Bertha bitterly exclaimed. "Hickok showed me one of those funny maps of yours. They're real good at telling you the names of streets and the like, but they don't let you know whose turf you're on, or which areas are most likely to get raided. When you get right down to it, them maps don't tell you shit! You count on your maps, and I can guarantee you you'll be wasted before a day is out."

"The Family needs the equipment and supplies on the list Plato gave me," Blade reminded her.

"Can't you find the stuff somewhere else?" Bertha pleaded. "Like you did that generator?"

Blade knew she was referring to the generator taken from the Watcher station in Thief River Falls, currently being stored in D Block. "It isn't that easy," he replied. "Plato and the Elders need specialized scientific and medical equipment. The Twin Cities have several major hospitals and the University of Minnesota. They have probably been ransacked since the Big Blast, but there is always the off chance some of the equipment we require is still there. Thanks to the hundreds of thousands of books Kurt Carpenter stocked in the Family library, many dealing with medicine, chemistry, and related fields, we possess the knowledge necessary to indicate probable causes for the premature senility affecting the Family. What we lack, and desperately must find, is the equipment essential to accurately pinpointing the reason for the senility. We certainly can't manufacture the equipment, leaving us one recourse. We must go out into the world and find it."

"Sometimes," Bertha said when Blade stopped speaking, "you use a lot of big words, just like Plato. I have a hard time following you."

"Sorry," Blade apologized. "I keep forgetting you never attended a school. The Family has a fine school, taught by the Elders. Plato is just one of the teachers. He takes personal pleasure in cultivating our vocabulary. Even Hickok knows a lot of big words, although you wouldn't know it from the way he usually talks."

"Ain't he somethin', though," Bertha stated proudly.

"You two are getting pretty close, I take it?" Blade ventured.

Bertha's lovely face clouded. "Not as close as I'd like, Big Guy."

"Oh?" Blade was genuinely surprised.

"Tell me something," Bertha said, leaning toward him. "You've known Hickok a lot longer than I have. What's he up to?"

"Up to?"

"Yeah. You know how I feel about him. It's no secret. At first, I thought he felt the same way, but lately he's been shying away from me. I don't know why. Do you?" Bertha inquired hopefully.

Blade shook his head. "I haven't the slightest idea."

"Too bad." Bertha sighed and rested her head on the tree trunk.

"You do know about Joan, don't you?" Blade asked her.

Bertha nodded, frowning. "Yeah. Your Jenny told me about her. Hickok was head over heels over her."

"Then you must realize he might take a while to get over her death," Blade remarked.

"I can understand that," Bertha responded. "I'd expect it. No, the thing I'm talking about is something else. I don't know what it is, but I sense he's hiding something from me."

"Like what?"

"I wish I knew," Bertha said. "I can see it in his eyes sometimes, like he wants to tell me something. But he holds it back. It's not like him, and I'm worried."

"I'll talk with him," Blade promised. This was extremely odd. First Joshua, then Plato, and now Bertha. All three were concerned for Hickok's welfare.

"You will?" Bertha asked eagerly.

"Sure."

"Great!" Bertha grinned. "I know he thinks more of you, and Geronimo, than anyone else. He might open up to you. If he does, will you let me know what it is?"

"You'll be the first person I tell," Blade pledged.

"Good!" Bertha appeared relieved. "Worrying about him is the only dark spot in my life right now."

"I take it you don't miss Minneapolis and St. Paul?" Blade questioned her.

Bertha laughed.

"Stupid to even ask," Blade muttered. "You're really happy here then?"

Bertha gazed at a huge white cloud in the blue sky overhead. "This has been the happiest time of my life. I never knew people could be this way, so peaceful and friendly. No one has tried to kill me or eat me for six weeks. Incredible! I keep thinkin' this is all a dream, and any second now I'll wake up and find a Wack chewing on my foot."

"The Wacks eat other people?" Blade asked, amazed.

"I told you the Wacks are crazy," Bertha replied. "The Porns aren't much better, to tell you the truth. I should know. I used to be one before I joined the Nomads."

"Now let me see if I remember what you said," Blade stated, thoughtfully recalling her words, "about these groups in the Twin Cities. Each of them has its own territory, its turf as you call it. The Nomads, the ones you belonged to before the Watchers caught you, are made up of former Porns and Horns, of people who are tired of the constant fighting."

"You got it," Bertha confirmed. "Zahner, the head of the Nomads, is the brains behind our group. Without him, I think the Nomads would fall apart."

"You said you call him Z, didn't you?"

"That's what we call him," Bertha verified. "I like him a lot, and I feel real bad betrayin' him the way I've done."

"You betrayed Zahner?" Blade queried her.

Bertha bit her lower lip and nodded. "Yep. Z sent me out to see if there was a way past the Watchers. They don't let anyone out of the Twins. But we can't take it there, no more. Z figures there has to be a way all of the Nomads can escape from the Twins and find a nice place to live, a place like this."

"And Zahner was relying on you to return with the information," Blade concluded.

"You got it." Tears filled Bertha's eyes. "And I can't do it! I can't go back there! Never again!"

Blade turned away, reflecting. How could he attempt to force her to return to the Twin Cities? The prospect apparently horrified her. Sure, having her along would make the trip easier and facilitate their search, but how could he justify compelling her to confront a nightmare she'd rather forget? And what if she were killed on the trip? Would he be able to live with himself?

"It's been nice talking with you," Blade announced, rising. "Hope I didn't upset you too much."

"You're leaving?" Bertha's surprise registered on her face.

"I've got to prepare for our departure," Blade explained. He began to walk off.

"You aren't going to try and talk me into going with you?" Bertha asked incredulously.

"Nope."

"Aren't you going to tell me I owe it to Hickok to make sure he gets in and out of the Twins safely?" Bertha pressed him.

"Nope."

"But I know the Twins like the back of my hand," Bertha added. "I can help you avoid the real dangerous parts."

Blade stopped and glanced over his left shoulder, smiling. "You stay here. We'll do all right. We're Warriors, remember?"

"You're a bunch of dummies," Bertha retorted. "You made a heap of mistakes in Thief River Falls."

"We'll survive," Blade said. "We don't need you."

"I could get the Nomads to help us," Bertha offered.

"You stay here."

"You don't stand a chance without me!" Bertha rose to her knees.

"We'll manage." Blade took several more steps.

"I'm going!" she yelled.

Blade faced her. "What did you say?"

"You heard me. I'm going."

"No, you're not," Blade stated.

"Bet me, sucker!" Bertha defied him.

"Look," Blade began, moving toward her. "I don't want you to come. Really!"

"I'm coming anyway."

Blade reached her side and stared into her eyes. "Why? Why change your mind so suddenly?"

"You talked me into it," Bertha replied.

"I did what?"

"You really are one clever son of a bitch, you know that?" She grinned at him.

"What?" Maybe, Blade speculated, he was the one who was dreaming!

"You knew I'd have to say yes," Bertha was saying. "I owe it to Zahner, and I owe it to you guys, and I mostly owe it to myself. You knew that all along."

"Sometimes," Blade said, shaking his head and strolling away, "I'm so brilliant, it's scary!"

Bertha, apprehensive over her decision, watched as the muscle-bound hunk headed toward the Blocks. What had he meant by that last crack? He was ten yards from her when he began laughing uncontrollably.

Now what's that all about? she wondered.

5

In the southeast corner of the Home, far from the Blocks and the cabins and the other areas where the Family normally congregated, was a section devoted to an exclusive purpose: the Family firing range. The children were taught to stay away from this area unless accompanied by an adult. Although it was utilized almost exclusively by the Warriors, the other members of the Family were required to take periodic firing lessons, to familiarize themselves with the proper use of firearms in case the Home was ever the target of a mass assault.

His hands hanging loosely at his sides, the buckskin-clad gunman concentrated on the six small sticks, each six inches in height, stuck in the dirt fifteen yards distant.

They were Trolls.

Six lousy Trolls, he told himself. Six of the rotten bastards responsible for killing his dear Joan. And they had to pay! Their lives were forfeit. Joan must be avenged!

His hands flew to his Colts, and the Pythons cleared leather simultaneously. The firing range rocked with the blasts of the six shots, and each of the sticks split at the middle as the slugs tore them in half.

"Piece of cake."

He twirled the Colts backwards into their respective holsters. His wounds were healed, and he was back in top form. If he stayed on his toes, and avoided being injured in the Twin Cities, he would implement his plan after they returned to the Home. Some of the Trolls had escaped during the course of the battle in Fox. Some of Joan's murderers were out there somewhere, free as a lark, unrepentant and unpunished.

They wouldn't be for long!

"That was some shooting," someone said behind him. "What they say about you is true, Hickok."

Hickok turned, annoyed by the intrusion on his thoughts, on his plotting for revenge.

The newcomer was dressed in black pants and a black shirt, both worn and faded and patched in a half-dozen places. His hair and eyes were brown, his face youthful and full with large cheeks and bushy brows. He wore a revolver around his waist.

"Don't I know you, boy?" Hickok asked, striving to recall the lad's name. It was on the tip of his tongue.

The youth reddened. "I'd appreciate it, Hickok, if you don't call me boy." He said the last word distastefully.

Hickok admired his pluck. "How would you like to be called?"

"Call me Shane."

The name was familiar. Hickok's favorite section of the library was the one filled with westerns. He remembered reading a book about a gunfighter named Shane, an outstanding novel dealing with life in the Old West, Hickok's favorite period in history.

"I wasn't aware we had anyone in the Family called Shane," he told the youth.

Shane hooked his thumbs in his belt, appearing slightly embarrassed. "Well, it's not really Shane yet," he said in explanation. "But it will be!" he hastily added. "My Naming is next week, and I intend to pick Shane."

"Aren't you Blake?" Hickok asked him. "Poe's son?"

Shane nodded, frowning. "Yeah. But I don't like to be called Blake."

"Fair enough, pard." Hickok extended his right hand and they shook. The boy's grip was firm and steady. "What can I do for you?"

"I heard you were leaving again," Shane stated.

"Soon," Hickok acknowledged.

"Then I'll make this short," Shane said. "I want to be a Warrior, like you. My father objects, and he refuses to sponsor me before the Elders. I know they're in the process of picking three new Warriors for another Triad, and I want to be one of them."

"So where do I fit in?" Hickok wanted to know.

"I want you to sponsor me," Shane answered.

"Forget it." Hickok began reloading the spent cartridges in his Pythons.

"What? Why?" Shane demanded defensively.

"Not my affair," Hickok succinctly replied.

"How do you figure?" Shane's disappointment was carved into his features.

"You just said your own father doesn't want you to become a Warrior," Hickok responded. "I'm not about to become involved in a family squabble. It's none of my affair."

"Yes it is," Shane asserted.

"Oh? How?"

"I've wanted to be a Warrior since I can remember. I'm not much good at building things, and farming bores me to tears. But I just know I'm cut out to be a Warrior, and I can prove it if I'm just given the chance," Shane said eagerly.

"You still haven't told me how I fit into all this," Hickok pointed out.

"It's simple." Shane stared into Hickok's eyes. "You're my hero."

Hickok, taken aback, laughed. "I'm what?"

"In school," Shane began, "we were taught the value of having heroes, of looking up to someone who does something you want to do very well. Face it. You have a reputation as one of the best Warriors in our Family, as one of the better Warriors the Family has ever had."

"I do not." It was Hickok's turn to feel a twinge of embarrassment.

"I'm not buttering you up," Shane stated. "Oh, Blade and Rikki and Geronimo and the rest are good Warriors, but it's you the Family talks about the most. Didn't you know that?"

"Sure didn't," Hickok replied.

"Well," Shane continued, "when I decided to become a Warrior, I naturally looked around to see which of the Warriors I would most like to emulate. Guess who I selected?" He smiled.

Hickok's Colts were reloaded, his hands resting on the grips. "I'm flattered, Shane. I truly am. But I still won't sponsor you for the new Triad."

"Why? What's wrong with me?" Shane's tone was plaintive.

"How do I know you can handle being a Warrior?"

"Who sponsored you?" Shane suddenly changed the subject.

"Blade's father," Hickok answered, recollecting his Naming. "My father had already passed on."

"And how did Blade's father know you could

handle being a Warrior?" Shane threw Hickok's own words back at him.

The gunman inadvertently grinned. "He trusted me."

"Don't you trust me?" Shane testily inquired.

Hickok started walking toward the western portion of the Home, Shane at his side. "I don't know you. How can I trust you?"

Shane fell silent for a moment, thinking.

"Don't take it personal, pard," Hickok advised him.

"What if I could do something to earn your trust?" Shane eagerly asked.

"Like what?"

"You tell me."

Hickok watched a hawk circle over a nearby field. "I can't think of a way, offhand."

"Try harder!"

"You sure are pushy for such a . . . young person," Hickok commented.

Shane grabbed Hickok's right arm. "Don't you realize how important this is to me? They don't pick new Warriors ever day, you know. I may not get another chance for years! You've got to help me!"

Hickok smiled at his aspiring protege. "I'll try and come up with something."

"You promise?"

"I promise."

"You won't regret it!" Shane was bubbling with enthusiasm. "I have a good head on my shoulders. I take orders real well. And I'm almost as good a marksman as you."

The last comment brought Hickok up short. "You think so, do you?"

"I know so," Shane stated confidently.

Hickok glanced around and spotted a dead tree thirty yards away. A pair of withered limbs hung at waist level on the right side of the trunk. "You see those branches on that dead tree?" He pointed.

Shane followed the direction his arm indicated. "Yep. You want me to hit them?"

"Tell you what we'll do," Hickok said. "I'll count to three. When I hit three, we'll both draw and fire. You take the top branch, I'll take the bottom. Okay with you?"

Shane's hefty frame coiled as he tensed, his right hand dangling above his revolver, an Abilene Single Action in .44 Magnum. "I'm ready when you are."

"That's a big gun you've got there, pard," Hickok observed. "You sure you can handle it?"

"Just do the counting," Shane replied, nervously flexing his right hand.

The dead tree was northwest of their position.

Smiling, pleased his ruse was working, Hickok let his hands drop to his side. "Okay, pard. Get ready."

"I was born ready!"

"One . . ." Hickok counted.

Shane froze, every muscle immobile, focused on the tree.

"Two. . . ." Hickok wondered if the youth would fall for it. If he did, Shane could forget being a Warrior.

"Three!" Hickok yelled, pretending to draw his Pythons.

Shane's hand was a streak as he whipped out the Abilene and cocked the hammer. His finger was tightening on the trigger when he abruptly stopped and glanced at Hickok.

The Warrior was standing quietly, waiting.

"You didn't draw!" Shane declared. "You didn't even draw!"

"And you didn't shoot," Hickok mentioned. "Why not?"

Shane looked at his revolver, then replaced it in its

holster. "You almost had me!" He breathed a sigh of relief.

"What do you mean?"

"Don't play innocent with me!" Shane barked. "The whole thing was a test, wasn't it?"

"Was it?"

Shane slapped his right thigh and laughed. "You're good. You are really good!"

"Am I?" Hickok asked quietly.

"You know as well as I do," Shane said, "that shooting inside the Home is only permitted on the firing range. Even the Warriors must follow this rule. The only exception is when the Home is under attack."

"Is that all?" Hickok queried.

"No, it isn't," Shane replied. "That dead tree is between us and the Blocks, where most of the Family is likely to be. If one of us had missed the tree, our bullet might have struck one of the Family."

"I'm impressed," Hickok admitted.

"Then it was a test?"

"Of course."

Shane stared from the tree to Hickok and back again. "But what if I had fired?"

"I would have stopped you," Hickok informed him.

"Oh? How?"

Hickok pointed at the Abilene. "Draw and fire at the tree."

"What?" Shane asked doubtfully.

"Draw as fast as you can," Hickok instructed him, "and try to shoot before I stop you."

"Nobody is that fast," Shane stated. "You'll never be able to stop me."

"Draw."

Shane instantly obeyed, his hand dipping and

bringing the gun up as he had hundreds of times in practice. The revolver was almost level when something caused the gun to abruptly jerk downward.

Hickok's right hand was on the Abilene, his palm pressing on the hammer, preventing Shane from firing.

Shane, astonished, gaped at the Warrior. "I can't believe it! I thought I was fast on the draw."

"You are," Hickok verified, releasing the Abilene and resuming his course toward the Blocks and the SEAL.

"But you beat me!" Shane protested.

"You're fast," Hickok repeated, "but being fast isn't enough."

"What more is there?" Shane asked, sliding the Abilene into its holster on his right hip.

"Quick."

"Quick? I don't understand," Shane frankly admitted.

"How can I explain it to you?" Hickok thought a moment. "Would you say a fly is fast?"

"A fly?"

"Yeah, pard, a fly. When it's buzzing around your head and you're trying to swat it, but you keep missing. Would you say that fly is fast?" Hickok glanced at the youth.

"I guess so," Shane said. "Flys can be hard to hit, hard to catch, sometimes."

"So imagine this same fast fly makes the fatal mistake of flying too close to a bullfrog sitting on the bank of a pond," Hickok elaborated. "The bullfrog snags the fly in its mouth and swallows it. What does that make the bullfrog?"

"Faster than the fly." Shane beamed.

"No."

"No?"

Hickok shook his head and stared at Shane. "It

makes the bullfrog quick. The fly may be fast, but the bullfrog is quick, and quick will win out over fast almost every time. You think about it."

"I will," Shane pledged.

They walked in silence for several minutes. The line of cabins in the center of the Home, the cabins used by the married couples and their families, came into view.

"So will you sponsor me, or not?" Shane spoke up.

"Let's say I'll give it serious consideration," Hickok replied.

Shane could barely contain his excitement. "You will? You really will?"

"A man should always keep his word," Hickok said solemnly. "And I do my best to keep mine. I'll think about sponsoring you on the way to the Twin Cities, and I'll give you my answer after I get back."

"Oh," Shane responded, frowning.

"What's wrong with you?"

"It's just . . ." Shane hesitated, reluctant to complete the sentence.

"Spit it out, hombre," Hickok urged him.

"How do I know you'll even make it back?" Shane blurted out. "Couldn't you speak to the Elders before you leave?"

"Not enough time," Hickok told him. "Don't you worry. I'm coming back. There's something I've got to tend to, and nothing is going to stop me."

"What is it?" Shane innocently asked.

"It's personal," Hickok growled.

"Oh," Shane said meekly, and then, to hastily change the subject, he added, "I was real sorry to hear about Joan."

Hickok's jaw muscles visibly tightened.

Shane, failing to notice Hickok's reaction, continued. "She was a nice person. Did you know I knew her?"

"What?" Hickok stopped and grabbed Shane's left wrist. "Are you making this up to impress me?"

"I wouldn't do that!" Shane retorted, hurt. "I really knew her. You see, I wanted to meet you, but I was a bit too shy to just walk up to you and introduce myself. Everyone was saying that Joan and you were . . . very close, and . . ." Shane stopped and glanced at his left wrist. "Are you trying to break it?"

Hickok self-consciously removed his hand.

"Anyway," Shane resumed, "like I was saying, I decided to ask Joan if she thought you would mind if I asked you a personal favor. She was so friendly and understanding . . ."

Hickok's mouth was a tight, tense line.

" . . . and she told me to go ahead, march right up to you and tell you what was on my mind. She said you'd admire me for having the guts to do it." Shane's voice lowered, assuming a sad tone. "But before I could follow her advice, the Trolls attacked the Home. She was one of their prisoners. I couldn't believe it when they said she was dead. I came to her funeral, but I don't think you noticed. It's taken me until now to muster up the courage to come see you." Shane looked up and saw Hickok's grim expression. "I'm sorry! Have I offended you?"

"No," Hickok muttered.

"I shouldn't of mentioned Joan," Shane realized. "I'm sorry . . ."

"It's not that," Hickok assured him, heading for the SEAL.

"Then what . . . ?" Shane asked, perplexed.

"It's the Trolls," Hickok revealed.

"The Trolls? I don't understand."

Hickok sighed. "We killed a lot of the bastards . . ."

"I heard you killed forty or fifty all by yourself,"

Shane interrupted.

"A slight exaggeration," Hickok stated.

"I also heard some of them got away," Shane commented.

"That's true," Hickok said, his voice barely audible, low and mean. "A couple of dozen, at least."

"For what they did to Joan," Shane remarked, "they don't deserve to live."

"They won't," Hickok vowed.

Shane thoughtfully studied the glowering gunman. What did Hickok mean by that last statement? Was he planning to retaliate against the Trolls still alive? How? No one knew where the Trolls had fled after the battle in Fox. Shane recalled Hickok saying he had "something I've got to tend to" after he returned from the Twin Cities. Was that it? Hickok was going after the Trolls!

"Listen, pard." Hickok faced Shane, smiling now. "Look me up after I get back. If you convince me you're worthy, I'll sponsor you. Fair enough?"

Shane, torn between disappointment and budding optimism, nodded.

"I've got to get my gear," Hickok announced, and walked off.

Shane watched the Warrior leave. Worthy? How in the world could he prove he was worthy? An idea suddenly occurred to him, and he was momentarily stunned by the brilliance of his inspiration. It was fantastic! If Hickok needed proof he was worthy, he would provide the proof, he would have it waiting for the gunman when Hickok returned. Shane grinned. If his deduction was correct, and Hickok intended to go after the Trolls, the Warrior would need to know where the Trolls were based, where their new headquarters was located. And wouldn't Hickok be impressed, Shane reasoned, if he had the information, and maybe a few bear-hide tunics too, when Hickok arrived after his trip to the Twin Cities!

Shane abruptly became aware of Hickok waving at him.

"Adios, pard!" Hickok yelled. "You keep practicing."

"You keep your head down!" Shane replied.

"You'll see me again," Hickok promised. "Next stop, the Twin Cities!"

6

It was the second day after their departure from the Home.

Blade was at the wheel, squinting from the glare of the afternoon sun, bright despite the tinted windshield. He kept the SEAL at a near steady rate of fifty miles an hour, carefully avoiding the many ruts and holes and cracks in the roadway. They were on Highway 59, cruising south. Fields and forest bordered the road.

"I'm glad we didn't stop for lunch," Hickok commented. "I can hardly wait to reach the Twin Cities."

Hickok, Bertha, and Joshua were sitting in the back seat. Their jerky, water, provisions, and ammunition were piled in the rear of the SEAL. Geronimo was sitting in the bucket seat across from Blade, studying their map.

"How much longer until we reach the Twin Cities?" Blade asked.

"Well, let's see." Geronimo ran his finger down the map, calculating their distance traveled and ascertaining the miles until the next town. "We've already passed Plummer and Brooks and Winger. A place called Bejou should be just ahead about a mile or so."

"I wonder if they will be as deserted as the others," Joshua speculated.

"Kind of funny we haven't seen any more Watchers," Hickok noted.

"That's not so unusual," Bertha chipped in.

"How do you mean?" Hickok asked her.

"As far as we know, the Watchers only keep posts in the larger towns and cities. You won't need to worry about runnin' into them until the next big town."

"The next town of any consequence," Geronimo informed them, his eyes glued to the map, "is a place called Detroit Lakes. Had about seven thousand at the time the war broke out."

"When will we reach it?" Blade wanted to know.

"Oh, it's between forty and fifty miles from where we're at right now," Geronimo answered. "At the speed you've been driving, we should reach it in an hour or so." He glanced at the watch on his left wrist, taken from a dead Watcher. "About three o'clock."

"I hope we do run into some more Watchers when we reach Detroit Lakes," Hickok said hopefully, adding in a low voice, "I have a score to settle and I aim to collect."

"You won't be collecting in Detroit Lakes," Blade informed Hickok.

"How come?"

"Because we'll be bypassing Detroit Lakes."

"Are you running from a good scrap?" Hickok asked, a touch of annoyance in his tone.

"You know better." Blade shook his head. "We've wasted enough time as it is. We simply can't afford another delay, and another fight with the Watchers might wind up with some of us being seriously hurt, or worse. Is there one of you who doesn't want to get back to the Home as quickly as we can?"

No one spoke.

"All right, then," Blade continued. "We already bypassed Thief River Falls, and we'll avoid any other potential Watcher outpost. The SEAL was constructed as an all-terrain vehicle, and it's time we put it to the test. We'll head around those towns possibly inhabited by the Watchers. That way, we should reach the Twin Cities without being attacked."

"Wait a minute, Big Guy," Bertha interjected. "You mean to tell me we are gonna cut across the country?"

"We certainly are."

"Lordy! I don't like that idea too much," Bertha protested. "We could run into the Uglies doin' that! Or worse!"

"We'll be protected inside the SEAL," Blade said.

"You hope."

"Don't worry."

"Who, me?"

"What about our meal this evening?" Geronimo questioned Blade. "Do you want me to bag some fresh meat?"

"No. We've got venison jerky and the canned food we took from the Watchers in Thief River Falls. When we run out of that, then you can hunt. We'll stop at night, for nature breaks, and that's it."

"You've got this all figured out, haven't you?" Bertha tried to catch a glimpse of Blade's face in the mirror.

"I do the best I can," Blade replied.

"I think you'll make a good Leader of your Family," Bertha expressed her opinion.

"What?" Blade cast a sharp glance in her direction.

"Hey! Don't get uptight, Big Guy. White Meat told me about you becoming the head of your Family some day."

"White Meat has a big mouth."

"What's eating you?" Bertha inquired.

"Nothing," Blade snapped. Plato's predecessor as Family Leader was Blade's father. Four years ago, after Blade's father had been brutally torn apart by a mutate, Plato had assumed the awesome responsibility of heading the Family. It was customary for Leaders to select their preferred successor and Plato, to Blade's extreme chagrin, had nominated him. Blade vividly remembered the difficulties and hardships his father had faced, and he wasn't certain he wanted the fate, the very lives, of over seventy people in his hands.

"Bejou ahead," Geronimo stated, staring down the highway.

Bejou turned out to be another deserted, dilapidated town, devoid of all signs of life and habitation. So did Mahnomen, Ogema, Callaway, and Westbury.

"About ten minutes till Detroit Lakes," Geronimo announced as they left Westbury behind.

"We'll find a spot to leave the road soon," Blade said.

Hickok, his head leaning against a window, was idly gazing up at the sky. He suddenly sat up. "What the blazes is that?"

"What's what?" Blade caught Hickok's reflection in the mirror.

"Stop the SEAL!" Hickok said urgently. "Get outside. Hurry!"

Without hestiation, Blade applied the brakes. He

opened his door, prepared to jump out.

"Up in the sky," Hickok stated. "Heading from north to south. Hurry!"

Blade ran around to the front of the SEAL, staring up at the blue sky. Geronimo joined him.

"What did he . . ." Blade began.

"I see it!" Geronimo raised his right arm, pointing.

"See what?"

"It's almost directly over us, bearing south. Do you see it yet?"

Blade did. A pinpoint of light streaking across the heavens on a southerly course.

"What is it?" Geronimo asked, fascinated.

"I don't know," Blade admitted.

"Do you hear something?" Geronimo cocked his head.

"No. Do you?"

"Yes. Can't quite describe it. Like a very faint hissing or buzzing. Never heard anything like it."

Blade and Geronimo stood rooted to the road, mesmerized as the dot of light continued to cross the sky.

"Then I wasn't imagining things!" Joshua had walked around in front of the transport.

"How do you mean?" Blade asked, keeping his eyes on the bright marvel approaching the southern horizon.

"I've seen that thing several times before."

"You have?" Blade glanced at Joshua. "When?"

"Oh, about three times in the past dozen years. Most of the time at night, when the light is much brighter. I prefer to worship at night, and I spend considerable time gazing at the stars, thanking and praising the Spirit."

"Why haven't you said something?"

Joshua shrugged. "What could I say? I did

mention a sighting to Plato once, and he expressed his belief that I'd seen a meteor or one of the satellites placed in orbit about the planet before the Big Blast. Hardly a cause for concern."

"Maybe." Blade thoughtfully stroked his chin. "Let's get back inside."

"What was it?" Hickok asked as they climbed back in. "Could it have been an aircraft of some kind?"

"We don't know," Blade replied. "If anyone should see it again, let me know."

"I've seen them before," Bertha chipped in.

"Oh?" Blade turned and faced her.

"Sure. They pass over the Twins every now and then. Sometimes at night, sometimes in broad daylight."

"Interesting," Blade commented. He resumed driving.

"Hey! Look at that! A lake!" Hickok exclaimed.

A large lake was visible to their east, the shore coming to within a couple of hundred yards of Highway 59.

"It's called Floyd Lake," Geronimo said, examining the map. "Or was," he amended.

"Too bad we can't do some fishing," Hickok said wistfully. "I like to fish."

"I've seen folks fish," Bertha commented, "but I never have."

"I'll show you some day." Hickok reached over and placed his hand on her shoulder. "You'll like it. It's real restful."

"Especially the way Hickok fishes," Geronimo quipped. "He never catches any. Just sits there, watching his line."

"Very funny," Hickok retorted. "Remind me to use you as bait next time."

Blade, waiting for his opportunity, swerved the

SEAL to his left, leaving Highway 59 behind, heading across the stretch of field between Floyd Lake and the road.

"What's your plan?" Geronimo inquired.

"We'll follow the western shore of the lake," Blade explained, "until we can bear due east. We'll make a half-circle around Detroit Lakes, and pick up Highway 59 on the other side. This way, we should avoid any entanglements with Watchers stationed in Detroit Lakes."

"Sounds good," Geronimo commented. "About ten miles past Detroit Lakes is a small town called Frazee, and twelve miles beyond that is one called Perham."

"We'll stop at Perham for the night," Blade said.

The map rustled as Geronimo spread a folded section open. "Wait a minute . . ."

"Is something wrong?" Blade spotted a rabbit hopping away from the SEAL.

"We don't pick up Highway 59 on the other side of Detroit Lakes."

"We don't?"

"No." Geronimo bent over the map. "Detroit Lakes is at a junction of several highways. On the other side of Detroit Lakes, Highway 59 heads toward the southwest."

"And we need to go the southeast," Blade stated.

"I know. Let me see." Geronimo was busy comparing symbols on the map. "The road we want to pick up beyond Detroit Lakes is called U.S. Highway 10."

"It takes us to the southeast?"

"Yep. As a matter of fact, it runs all the way into the Twin Cities." Geronimo looked up, smiling. "We're getting there, slowly but surely."

"I hope this U.S. Highway 10 is in good shape," Blade said.

"Should be. According to this map, U.S. Highway 10 is something called a four-lane divided highway. It appears to be a wider road than Highway 59."

"And we'll have it all to ourselves," Hickok mentioned. "I'm beginning to like this driving business. It's fun."

"So long as we don't run into one of the Watcher's vehicles," Bertha absently commented.

"That's a risk we'll just have to take," Blade remarked.

"I just hope," Bertha stated, "you guys do better in the Twin Cities than you did in Thief River Falls."

"What's that crack supposed to mean?" Hickok questioned her.

"How soon we forget!"

"Forget what?" Hickok pressed her.

Bertha looked at each of them, shaking her head. "What a bunch of dummies!"

Hickok grinned. "I know what you mean, and excluding myself I think you're right."

"You're included, bozo," Bertha informed him.

"In what?"

"Who was it," Bertha asked, "who fed the dead Watchers to the rats in Thief River Falls?"

"We did," Hickok admitted sheepishly.

"To be precise," Geronimo interjected, "I did."

Bertha nodded knowingly. "And we were almost overrun by the damn things!"

"So we made one small mistake," Hickok conceded.

"And who was it," Bertha added, "who thought the Watchers might be friendly? What a bunch of dummies!" she repeated, laughing.

Blade was frowning. "She's right, you know."

"What do you mean?" Geronimo asked.

"We keep making stupid assumptions, basing our

actions on our past experience, experience that's inadequate when compared to the new realities we're encountering away from the Home. Bertha is entirely correct."

"What'd he say?" Bertha wanted to know.

"He said we're dummies," Hickok explained.

"I already said that," Bertha reminded them.

"How were we to know that rats lived under Thief River Falls?" Geronimo said, defending their actions. "How are we to know what we'll encounter out here? Just how were we supposed to know about the Brutes? You can't fault us for our ignorance."

"I just pray our ignorance doesn't cost us a life," Blade said sadly.

"Life is eternal," Joshua chimed in, "if you have living faith. Even if one of us is killed, we will pass on to the mansions on high. 'I am come a light into the world, that whosoever believeth on me should not abide in darkness,' " he quoted from John.

"All well and good," Blade said. "But I'd still prefer to get all of us back to the Home in one piece. I just wish there was a way to minimize our mistakes."

"Life is a learning experience," Joshua replied., "We learn by doing. Unfortunately, some of the lessons we must learn can only be derived from bitter experience. Have faith, Blade! All will come out for the good of the Spirit in the end."

Blade concentrated on his driving.

The countryside was changing. Around the Home, the vegetation was lush, the forest thick with trees and brush. The same held true for Thief River Falls, its park and other natural areas. The terrain near Detroit Lakes, however, was different. The trees were sparser, shorter and gnarled. Tall grass, waving in the wind, surrounded Floyd Lake.

"This is prime grazing country," Hickok commented.

"Too bad we don't have some cattle," Geronimo said, lamenting the Family's misfortune.

"The Family would be delighted if we could return with a cow," Blade agreed.

"What's a cow?" Bertha asked.

"That's a cow!" Hickok said, excited, pointing.

Blade slowed.

Several hundred yards distant, near the southern shore of Floyd Lake, grazed a small herd of cattle.

"I don't believe it!" Hickok pressed his face against the SEAL. "Must be twenty, thirty head out there. Do we stop and try to capture one?"

"No. We can't spare the time. Maybe on our way back from the Twin Cities," Blade answered.

"What kind of cows are they?" Joshua asked.

"Beats me," Blade said. "But if they've been running wild all these years, I can see where catching one is going to be extremely difficult."

As if to accentuate his statement, the herd, having spotted the mechanical intruder, took off, following the shore of the lake towards the east.

The SEAL easily negotiated the rolling fields, circling Detroit Lakes. At one point, when they were bearing south, they crossed a pitted, worn road.

"Highway 34," Geronimo announced. "It runs east and west."

They maintained a southerly course until Blade was satisfied Detroit Lakes was well behind them. He turned west, and within three miles they came up on U.S. Highway 10. It turned out to be in the best condition of any roadway they had traveled on so far.

"It's incredible that these roads have survived this long," Geronimo mentioned.

"I recall reading in the library," Joshua said, "that roads built by an ancient civilization called the Romans were still in existence, some even being used, at the time of the Big Blast."

Blade had a thought. "Say, Bertha?" he called to her.

"Yeah, Big Guy?"

"You're familiar with the Twin Cities?"

"I know my way around pretty good. I should. I've lived there all my life. You know that. Why ask such a dumb question?"

Blade grinned at her frankness. "What I meant was, how well do you know what's in the Twin Cities? What buildings are there and even more importantly, what's inside those buildings?"

"Well," she said, scratching her head, "I know the north and west parts of the Twins pretty good. The north part is Nomad turf, and I used to be a Porn, so I know the west real good. The south part is where the Wacks hole up, and nobody goes there unless they've got a death wish, so even the Porns don't use it that much. I ain't never been in the east part. That's Horn turf, enemy territory. Why you askin' these questions?"

"You know we must find certain types of scientific and medical equipment," Blade answered. "Can you think of any buildings that might house what we need?"

"Scientific and medical equipment?" Bertha repeated doubtfully. "Don't rightly know what you're talkin' about, but I might be able to help some." She thought a minute. "Most of the Twins, you gotta understand, was trashed long ago, right after the war. In the center of the Twins is an area that doesn't rightfully belong to anybody. It's kind of a no-man's-land. Least that's what it's called. You might find what you're lookin' for there, though you'd be crazy to go in there."

"What makes you think we'll find what we need there?" Blade asked her.

"I've been there, once or twice," she said grimly. "There's some big buildings called hospitals there, and one part, Zahner told me, used to be what they called a university. There's a bunch of signs that call it the University of Minnesota. Aren't they what you told me you were looking for?"

Blade smiled. "That sounds exactly like what we need."

"You boys is nuts!"

"Why do you say that?"

"Cause a lot of the Wacks is there, and the Lone Wolves, and worse. The Wacks come up out of the tunnels. They're based in the south, but you never know where they'll appear. The Porns and the Horns and the Nomads are always sendin' patrols in that area. You try going in there, you'll wind up dead. I know I ain't going in there!"

"You won't have to," Hickok assured her.

"No," Blade added. "You just point us in the right direction and we'll take care of the rest."

"Another town up ahead," Geronimo announced.

This one was a small town called Frazee, abandoned and disintegrating from the decades of neglect and abuse from the elements.

"We'll keep going," Blade said as they drove through the former business section. "I want to put more distance between Detroit Lakes and us. What was the name of the next town?"

"It's named Perham," Geronimo responded. "Had two thousand inhabitants before the Big Blast."

"We'll stop there for the night."

"But it will still be light," Geronimo pointed out. "Shouldn't we take advantage of the light and keep traveling?"

"I'm thinking of all of us," Blade replied. "We must all be rested when we enter the Twin Cities."

"We're okay, pard," Hickok said.

"Don't stop on account of us," Bertha stressed.

"I am stopping on account of us," Blade reiterated. "We'll be refreshed when we reach the Twins. A good sleep will help immensely." Blade turned to Geronimo. "When do you think we'll reach the Twin Cities?"

Geronimo spent several minutes computing, correlating the information presented on the map. "If my calculations are correct, and bear in mind this is a rough estimate . . ." He tapped the map, reviewing his data. "Keeping in mind Blade's speed, which has been hovering at fifty miles per hour, and taking into account detours to avoid possible Watcher stations, and . . ."

"Will you just answer the blasted question?" Hickok interrupted. "You're beginning to sound like Plato!"

" . . . and subtracting time for potty breaks, we should reach the Twin Cities . . ." Geronimo glanced up, smiling. "By tomorrow night."

"Yee-hah!" Hickok shouted.

"That soon?" Joshua asked.

"As near as I can tell," Geronimo confirmed.

"Back to the Twins," Bertha said apprehensively.

Blade looked at the speedometer. Maybe even sooner. He had picked up speed since encountering U.S. Highway 10. On Highway 59, which had been considerably narrower, and in rougher condition, he'd kept the SEAL at close to fifty miles per hour. But he should be able to average sixty on U.S. Highway 10, just as he was doing now, all the way to the

74

Twin Cities if their luck held. The SEAL was capable of much greater speeds, but Blade was reluctant to open the vehicle up. He still entertained lingering doubts about his driving ability, and they couldn't afford to damage the SEAL through his carelessness.

"Back to the Twins," Bertha said again. She shuddered.

Hickok placed an arm around her shoulders. "Don't worry, Black Beauty. We're not staying there long. Am I right, Blade?"

"You're right." Blade nodded. "I want to get in and out as fast as we can."

"You see?" Hickok said to Bertha. "In and out. Easy as that."

"Bet me, sucker!"

7

The SEAL stopped at the crest of a long, sloping grade. Below them, a quarter mile distant, loomed huge black monoliths, towering over an obscured jumble of lesser buildings, the entire scene shrouded in darkness, conveying an eerie, sinister air.

"Lordy!" Bertha exclaimed in a whisper. "I'm back at the Twins."

"The Twin Cities," Blade said as quietly as Bertha. "We've made it."

"Why the blazes are you whispering?" Hickok asked in his usual tone of voice.

"Why is it so dark down there?" Joshua inquired, before they could respond to Hickok.

"What'd you expect, sugar?" Bertha glanced at Joshua. "We ain't got any electricity down there. Only fire. And we only keep fires on our own turf, hidden from view, under guard. You start a fire out in the open, and the first thing you know, you've attracted all kinds of trouble! We go down there tonight, we go down in the dark."

"Are we going in tonight?" Geronimo asked Blade.

76

Blade leaned back in his seat, deliberating.

The SEAL was stopped, the engine off, on Highway 47, just north of the Twin Cities. They had reached their destination! Finally! Blade's mind raced, recalling their progress since dawn.

They had risen early that morning, everyone excited at the prospect of reaching the Twin Cities before the day was done. As he had done every morning of their trip, Blade had remembered to throw the red lever under the dash to the right. An hour later, after the SEAL was fully energized, he would position the lever in the center. They had eaten hastily, eager to begin their travel. Bertha had become strangely subdued, reluctant to talk, preoccupied with thoughts of returning to the dreaded Twins. Hickok had attempted to cheer her up, to no avail. Her sullen, apprehensive attitude had begun to affect the others, except for Hickok.

While Bertha withdrew into herself, Hickok had opened up, loquacious, enthusiastic about the adventures ahead. His sense of excitement had served as an effective counterbalance to Bertha's somber demeanor. Each of them had carefully checked their weapons, insuring their firearms were cleaned and loaded.

Blade had pushed the SEAL that day, frequently reaching speeds of over sixty miles an hour on straight stretches. They had left Perham an hour after sunrise. In rapid succession, they had passed through more abandoned towns: New York Mills, Bluffton, Wadena, Verndale, Aldrich, Staples, and Motley. At Lincoln, they had made a temporary detour, driving to Crookneck Lake for a food break and a bath. The men had bathed in one secluded cove, Bertha in another. Blade and Hickok had shaved Family style by scraping the sharp edge of a knife across their skin. Joshua, sporting a full beard, never bothered with shaving. Geronimo, too, never worried about facial hair. Years ago, when his beard and moustache first began to grow in, he had plucked the hairs, one by one, Indian fashion, from his skin. Now his face was completely devoid of hair, except for his brows.

Their ablutions completed, they had rejoined U.S. Highway 10, heading south. They had circled around Little Falls, wary it might be a Watcher station, and had passed through Royalton and Rice. Again, exercising caution, they had wasted more time bypassing St. Cloud. Bertha, visibly upset by the memories, had informed them that she had been captured by the Watchers near St. Cloud and held there for almost a week before being passed on to another Watcher station.

"I won't tell you what them bastards did to me," she had said, her voice low and strained.

"No need," Hickok had assured her. "And don't you worry! We'll pay them back for what they did to you."

"How are we gonna make 'em pay?" she had asked. "There's too many for us to kill every Watcher."

"Leave it to me," Hickok had stated confidently. "We'll think of something."

Bertha had grinned half-heartedly. "I bet you will, White Meat. I just bet you will."

Additional small towns had faded into the distance behind them. Cable, Clear Lake, Clearwater, Becker, and Big Lake. Elk River, the last distinct town, had now been left behind.

Blade's thoughts came back to the present. He started the SEAL. They entered the suburbs of Minneapolis as the sun was vanishing beyond the horizon.

"This is Anoka," Bertha announced as row after

row of single-family residences flashed by. "It's on the outskirts of Nomad turf. It's ours, but we don't keep any people in it. Just patrol it from time to time. It's a good place for huntin'. So's Coon Rapids."

Coon Rapids was the next area they slowly crossed.

"I expected to see more people," Hickok commented.

"What people?" Bertha rejoined. "There ain't that many left in the Twins as it is. Maybe a couple of thousand, if that many."

"Where did the population go?" Joshua inquired.

"Don't rightly know, sugar," Bertha replied.

"They were probably evacuated after the Big Blast," Blade mentioned. "Just like all the other towns we've seen."

"Then how come there are still some folks left here?" Hickok asked. "We know from our records the Government ordered them out."

"They might have been in a rush," Blade offered. "Besides, you couldn't expect them to round up every person in a city of this size. Maybe some people hid out, maybe they didn't want to be evacuated from their homes. Who knows?"

"What I'd like to know," Geronimo said, joining in their speculation, "is where everyone was evacuated to. That's the big question."

"Maybe we'll find the answer to that some day," Blade said. "Right now, we've got more important issues to decide. For instance, what's this intersection coming up?"

Geronimo brought the map close to his eyes, squinting to read in the fading light. "The map says U.S. Highway 10 intersects with State Highway 47."

"And where does this State Highway 47 go?"

Geronimo smiled. "Directly into the center of the Twin Cities," he answered. "At least, into the heart of Minneapolis. St Paul is further east."

"Then it sounds like 47 is just what we need," Blade said. He wheeled the SEAL onto State Highway 47.

Bertha was staring out the side of the SEAL. "I know where I am," she told them. "I know the landmarks!"

"Do you want us to let you out?" Blade asked her. He was having difficulty distinguishing the road because of the gathering darkness. "If this is Nomad territory, it's your home. Would you rather return to your friends?"

"I told you before," Bertha snapped, "I ain't never going back to the Nomads! I didn't even want to come back here!"

"Just asking."

The SEAL was moving through Fridley.

"I can't see a thing," Joshua commented.

"Shouldn't we stop?" Geronimo asked Blade.

"We keep going."

Geronimo twisted in his seat, scanning their surroundings. He was sitting in the bucket seat across from Blade. Hickok, Bertha, and Joshua were in the back seat. After their break at Crookneck Lake, they had piled all the supplies in the rear section again.

"I've got a real bad feeling about this," Bertha announced in a trembling voice.

They drove under an overpass.

"That was Interstate Highway 694," Geronimo stated.

"Still no sign of anyone, pard," Hickok said.

The homes they were passing were bigger now, obviously grander. A small sign read COLUMBIA HEIGHTS. The road gradually followed an extended incline. They reached the top and stopped.

"The Twin Cities!" Hickok yelled, pointing ahead.
The inner city rose in front of them.

And now they were anxiously perched on the edge
of their seats, waiting for Blade's decision.

"Are we going in tonight?" Geronimo repeated.

"Maybe we should spend the night in the SEAL
and get some rest," Blade said.

"Who can sleep, pard?" came from Hickok.

"I just want to get out of here," Bertha said,
expressing her opinion.

"I'm too excited to rest," Joshua remarked.

"It might be best to go in under cover of night."
Blade formulated his plans aloud for their benefit.
"We'd have less chance of being spotted and inter-
fered with. We could go in, find the buildings we're
looking for, ascertain if the equipment we need is
actually there, and get out again. Quick and neat.
What do the rest of you think?"

"Piece of cake," Hickok cracked. "I say we go for
it!"

"I'll follow whatever you say," Geronimo said.

"You are the Warrior," Joshua stressed. "You are
the Triad Leader. I will follow you."

Blade turned, looking at Bertha. "Haven't heard
from you yet," he goaded her. "Your opinion
matters the most. You'll be the one leading us in
there."

"What if I decide to stay right here?" she said
defiantly. "What if I stay put in the SEAL and let
you go on alone?"

"That's your prerogative," Blade informed her.

"My what?"

"He means it's up to you," Hickok explained.
"You can do whatever you want to do."

"You got that straight!" Bertha said. She noticed
Hickok's brow was creased, his eyes searching her

81

face. "What's the matter with you, White Meat? Why're you lookin' at me that way?"

Hickok shook his head. "I never took you for yellow."

"What?"

"I never would have thought you're a coward."

Bertha reacted before any of them could move to stop her. She brought her left hand up and across Hickok's mouth.

Hickok recoiled, more from surprise than pain. He touched his mouth with his right hand. "I reckon I had that coming."

Bertha averted her gaze, twisting to stare out of the transport. "I'm sorry," she quickly apologized, upset because she had lost control, and afraid it would happen again. "You're right."

"I am?"

"Yep." She pressed her forehead against the cool plastic. "Oh, God, help me!" she nearly whined. "I don't know what to do, White Meat! I don't know what to do!"

Hickok squeezed her shoulder in assurance. "We're here with you, Black Beauty. There's nothing to be afraid of."

Bertha spun on them. "But there is!" she shouted. "Can't you stupid sons of bitches see it yet? After all I told you? You just got no idea how bad it is out there! No idea!" She sagged against the seat. "And to think," she said to herself, "I was out. I was safe and free!"

"You can stay here," Blade told her. "We won't hold it against you."

Bertha glanced up at them, her eyes wet. "Maybe you guys wouldn't, but I'd hold it against myself." She tried a weak smile. "Besides, if we're going to die, it might as well be together."

"No one is going to die," Hickok said.

Bertha gently traced a finger along Hickok's mouth. "If you say so."

"Then it's settled," Blade declared. "We go in tonight and get this whole mess over with."

"On foot, or in the SEAL?" Geronimo asked.

"We'd be safer in the SEAL," Hickok pointed out.

"Safer," Blade agreed, "but conspicuous. The SEAL's engine is quiet, but it still makes noise that could be heard a block away. It's dark outside. There's no moon. If we used the lights we'd . . ."

"Lights?" Hickok cut him off. "We'd really draw attention to ourselves if we did that."

"As I was about to say," Blade continued, "before I was so rudely interrupted, if we used the lights on the transport, we'd be sending an invitation to everyone in the Twin Cities to come and check us out. Since attracting attention is the last thing we want to do, using our lights is positively out of the question. And although we would be safer in the SEAL, and the vehicle is bulletproof, it's not indestructible and could be damaged by attackers."

"So what's your plan?" Geronimo inquired.

"We take 47 to the next turn," Blade detailed, "find a spot to hide the SEAL, then proceed on foot. We'll try and find what we're looking for, and get back here by dawn. Bertha, you're the one guiding us. How does my plan sound to you?"

"Just wonderful," she said sarcastically.

"I'm serious."

"So am I."

"You don't think it will work?"

Bertha snickered. "If we were going by what I think, we wouldn't even be here right now."

"If you don't want to come . . ." Blade began.

"We've gone through that!" Bertha said angrily. "I'm comin' with you. As far as your bright idea goes, sure, it sounds great."

"Any suggestions you want to make?"

Bertha glared at Blade. She thought of one she wanted to make, but thought better of it. "No. Whatever you say sounds fine to me."

"Okay. Recheck your weapons." Blade started the SEAL and cautiously drove forward, at five miles an hour, seeking a secluded hiding spot for the transport.

The others went over their guns. Hickok had his Henry, Geronimo his Browning. Joshua had his pouch containing his Ruger Redhawk over his shoulders, and he was holding a Smith and Wesson shotgun in his hands, both provided by Blade with strict orders to carry them whether he liked the idea or not. Bertha had picked a Springfield Armory MIA, a rifle once owned by Watchers.

A stand of trees became dimly visible to their left, growing in the center of a field.

"Found what we need!" Blade angled the SEAL across the field and into the trees, driving far enough in to insure the vehicle would be safe from prying eyes. He reluctantly switched the ignition off. The SEAL provided a sense of security and an emotional link to the Family difficult to forsake, even briefly. "We'll lock the SEAL and head off, making for the center of the Twins." He grabbed his Commando from the console at his side.

"No-man's-land," Bertha said, shivering in the dark.

They climbed from the transport, Blade securing the doors. "It should be safe here," Blade whispered as he joined the others at the back of the SEAL, placing the keys in his right front pocket.

"We hope, pard."

Blade waved his arm and they crept through the trees until they reached the field. He scanned the field. The sky was moonless, the field cast in gloom, but some detail could still be differentiated.

"It's so quiet," Joshua murmured.

It was. No sound, except for the soft swishing of the leaves and the hissing of the wind.

Blade headed across the field, keeping his eyes on the black silhouettes of downtown Minneapolis. Some of those buildings appeared to be incredibly tall. What had they been called? A name from his studies came to mind: skyscrapers.

They reached State Highway 47.

Why not use it? Blade asked himself. They'd made good time, and it went directly into downtown Minneapolis. Just what they needed. Once they were there, Bertha could lead them to the places where they might find the items listed on the piece of paper in his left front pocket.

Blade led them at a trot, following 47 south. They came on an intersection marked by a bent, slightly rusted road sign. The top of the sign was dangling inches from the ground. Blade knelt by the sign, trying to read the imprint. Impossible. The paint on the lettering had long since worn off, and it was too dark to discern the names. He pressed his fingers against the sign, tracing the figures, a relatively easy task. They were at the intersection of 47th and 37th.

Geronimo crouched beside Blade. "I heard a sound," he whispered.

"What? Where?"

"Up there," Geronimo said, pointing ahead and to their left. "A deep grunt. Animal, I believe."

"Keep on your toes," Blade quietly directed the others as he stood and continued down 47th.

Two blocks elapsed. They passed several rows of former houses, each a vague blob in the darkness.

Blade spotted a wide area of vegetation to their left. The source of the animal grunt Geronimo heard? He gripped his Commando and peered into the night, seeking any intimation of movement.

Bertha grabbed Blade's right elbow and he stopped.

"I forgot to tell you about the dogs," she now informed him.

"Dogs?"

"Yeah. A lot of dog packs roam the Twins, hunting for anything they can eat. Including people."

Maybe, Blade mentally noted, when the Twin Cities were evacuated, a lot of people had left their pets behind to fend for themselves. If so, how big would the canine population be by now?

"There's other things," Bertha added as Blade began to move.

"Other things?"

"I don't know what you'd call 'em, or where they came from, but there's other animals that kill humans, animals worse than the dogs."

"Terrific."

Blade waved them on. They stayed close to one another, their eyes alert, their senses primed.

A guttural growl emanated from the trees to their left.

Blade froze, waiting, the others right behind him.

The trees came close to the road, perhaps twenty yards away. Something moved in the dense brush under the trees, the brush crackling as a large body squeezed a passage through the pressing limbs.

The breeze gained strength, changing direction, carrying their scent towards the trees.

The thing grunted.

Blade ran, the rest on his heels. Whatever it was, it had picked up their scent. If it was carnivorous, it would be after them in moments.

A savage snarl shattered the night behind them.

"Damn!" Blade halted, turning to face the way they had come.

Heavy pads pounded on the highway, coming at them.

"You keep going," Blade told the others. "I'll hold it off."

They didn't move.

"Did you hear me? I said to get out of here!"

Hickok grinned. "Since when did a Warrior desert another Warrior, pard? Especially one from his own Triad?" He raised his Henry to his shoulder.

"Hickok's right," Geronimo stated. "For once."

"Well, I sure ain't wanderin' off by myself," Bertha said.

Joshua smiled, the white of his teeth a contrast to the darkness engulfing them. "I can't leave you without spiritual guidance, can I?"

There was no time for Blade to argue.

The animal was fifteen yards distant when they distinguished a fluid form rushing at them on all fours. It snarled again as it closed in, voicing its hunger and anticipation.

Blade hesitated a fraction, adverse to advertising their presence by firing. Anyone, or anything, within miles would know they were there if they opened up.

There was no other option.

Blade let loose with the Commando, everyone firing on his cue. The din was almost deafening.

Whatever was charging them buckled and went down, crashing to the tarmac.

In the silence that followed, Blade could hear a ringing in his ears. They approached the thing slowly, their guns ready, their nerves taut.

The animal was convulsing, the brawny legs twitching, the tail jerking spasmodically.

"What the blazes was it?" Hickok asked.

Geronimo knelt and ran his hand along the blood-soaked pelt. "A big cat of some kind," he replied. "It's too dark to see these markings clearly." He studied the skin, trying to place the cat.

"It kind of resembles a mountain lion," Blade said softly.

"No." Geronimo shook his head. "What were they . . ." He hesitated, suddenly recalling a book in the Family library.

"Do you know what this is?" Bertha gawked at the giant feline.

"I've got it!" Geronimo exclaimed. "It's a leopard or a jaguar! It's got to be!"

"Naw, pard," Hickok objected. "Can't be. I read about them critters. They're not native to these parts."

"I remember reading about places where unusual animals were kept." Geronimo was probing his memory for the word he wanted. "They were displayed in barred cages, sometimes in fenced enclosures, in what were called . . ." He paused, the term eluding him.

"They were called zoos," Blade said, helping him, "and circuses."

"That's right. Maybe some of the animals got away or were set free after the war," Geronimo proposed. "Maybe some of the species survived until now."

"If that's true," Joshua interjected, "then we could, conceivably, encounter any manner of creature on this expedition."

"Just what we needed," Hickok said.

Blade raised his eyes to the multitude of stars overhead. What next? Watchers! Brutes! Big cats! There was just one obstacle after another! Would he ever see Jenny again? He wanted nothing more than to return to the safety of the Home and bind to the woman he loved with his heart and soul. Blade shook himself. This was not the time or place for romantic reverie.

"Let's go," he announced grimly, a resentment building within him, an animosity for anyone or anything that might try to come between him and his goal.

The quiet became oppressive.

They jogged along 47, listening for any trace of other life.

Hickok stayed alongside Bertha. He knew she was scared, and he admired her fortitude in coping with that fear and suppressing it so effectively. The girl had to be a survivor if she had lasted in the Twin Cities this long.

Joshua brought up the rear, constantly glancing over his shoulder. The gunfire might have scared off potential enemies, though he doubted it. The opposite could well be true. The shots might attract the Nomads or the Horns or the Porns. They might want to try to steal the firearms.

Geronimo kept pace with Blade. His eagle eyes probed the night. The Arminius was snug under his right arm, the tomahawks at his waist. He noticed a break in the road ahead and slowed.

Highway 47 rose in front of them, forming an overpass.

Geronimo glanced down, over the concrete abutment. Some sort of peculiar, narrow tracks ran under the overpass. What were they? he wondered.

Blade stopped at the top of the overpass. "We'll take a break," he stated.

"So far, so good," Hickok optimistically quipped.

"We got a long way to go, White Meat." Bertha leaned against the abutment.

"Bertha." Blade walked over to her. "Exactly how far?"

89

"Don't rightly know. Couple of miles."

"What's closer?" Blade stared out over the benighted city. "A hospital? A scientific building?"

"I told you before, honky," Bertha reiterated, "I ain't too sure about what you're lookin' for." She paused, took a deep breath, and blurted out, "I can't read."

"You what?" Blade turned on her.

"I can't read nor write a lick," she said sadly, her head bowed.

"Then how would you know what a hospital is?" Blade demanded. "And before you mentioned the University of Minnesota. How would you know it was a university?"

"Z told me. He's Nomad Leader, remember?"

"What?"

"Zahner. His parents taught him some readin' and writin' before they died. There's still a heap of signs up, tellin' us what everything was before the war. He's been tryin' to teach me, but I'm a slow learner."

"Don't worry none, babe," Hickok assured her. "When we get back to the Home, I'll teach you myself."

"You will?" she brightened. "I've always wanted to learn."

"Just don't ask him for driving lessons," Geronimo advised her.

"So what's closest?" Blade interrupted their banter, probing Bertha. "Where do we go from here?"

"We keep goin' on 47," she told him. "It becomes University Avenue. About three miles from where we're standin' is the University of Minnesota itself. It might be your best bet. There's a lot of big buildings used by smart types before the war. Oh," she added as an afterthought, "there's also three hospitals real close to one another."

"Three?"

"Yeah." She counted them off. "There's the University Hospital at the University, and a mile from that is one called Shriner's Hospital, and a ways east is one called Midway Hospital."

"Piece of cake," Hickok said.

"Maybe not."

"Why?"

" 'Cause all of this stuff is right in the middle of no-man's-land," she said, her voice on edge. "Not many people go there in the day, and no one's been stupid enough to go at night."

"Until now," Hickok corrected.

"Yeah. Just my dumb luck to be along when it's done."

Hickok laughed.

"Okay." Blade had decided. "We'll stay with this road all the way to the University of Minnesota. We'll run a mile, rest a bit, then run about another mile. I want us in top form when we get there."

"If we're not in top form now," Hickok joked, "we will be by the time we get there."

They ran in determined silence, eating up the distance. The buildings closed in on the highway the further they went. Taller structures, former businesses and offices and apartments, replaced individual houses with increasing frequency.

Blade found his mind straying. What would they do if they couldn't locate the supplies and equipment Plato required? What if their entire trip here was wasted? Their lives endangered, their futures in jeopardy, for what? He grinned. At the very least the Family had a new member and Hickok a new . . . friend. He knew Bertha liked Hickok, and he suspected the gunman reciprocated, but Bertha had intimated Hickok was holding back. Why?

A clanging sound momentarily split the shadows off to their right.

Blade whistled and dropped flat, braced. Hickok and Geronimo did likewise, Hickok pulling Bertha down, Geronimo grabbing Joshua.

The clanging stopped.

"Oh, Lordy!" Bertha whispered, terrified.

"What's the matter?" Hickok asked her. He could feel her shaking.

"The Wacks."

"The crazy ones you were telling us about?"

"None other. We're in for it, for sure!"

"We can handle them," Hickok promised her.

Bertha gently touched Hickok's right cheek. "If we don't get the chance to know one another more," she said softly, "I want you to remember I liked you a lot."

"What's with the past tense? We're still alive, and where there's life, there's hope."

"That's beautiful." Bertha smiled at him. "You got brains to go with your looks."

"I read it somewhere," Hickok said, embarrassed, "and I wish you'd stop complimenting me in public."

"I don't care who knows how I feel."

"Let's go," Blade ordered, moving out.

"Thank the Spirit!" Hickok muttered, following.

It took them thirty minutes to reach the junction of University and 10th.

"That's the place." Bertha pointed when they stopped in the intersection. "The things you want might be in there."

The college campus was a jumble of black buildings, stands of trees, and high weeds.

"Look at this," Joshua remarked. He walked to their left.

A rusted automobile stood at the side of the road. The windows were gone, the tires flat and frayed almost to nothing.

"There's a lot of them scattered around," Bertha explained.

"To be expected," Blade commented. He faced the University. Where should they begin? He didn't relish the idea of them groping around in the dark, and lighting torches would attract any undesirables in their vicinity. Maybe he'd made another mistake. Maybe they should have used the SEAL. Maybe they should have waited until morning. It wasn't too late to turn around, to go back to the transport and wait for daylight.

Or was it?

The metallic clanging sounded from the direction of the darkened buildings in front of them.

"It's the Wacks!" Bertha whispered, horrified. "I told you!"

"You sure?" Hickok asked her.

"It's the way they signal each other." Bertha nervously hefted the Springfield. "We're dead!"

Geronimo squatted on his haunches, peering into the night. The shadows appeared to be moving. "They're closing in," he warned the rest. "A lot of them." He glanced up at Blade.

Blade made up his mind. "Back to the SEAL," he directed them. "If we're separated, whatever else happens, get back to the SEAL."

"I don't know if I could find it," Joshua candidly admitted.

Suddenly, from not far away, a booming male voice called out a single word. "MUH-EET!"

"What the blazes was that?" Hickok whirled, his

Henry ready.

"MUH-EET!" came from the darkness.

"Sounds like someone saying the word 'meat,'" Joshua declared.

"MUH-EET!"

They could hear feet, many feet, shuffling in the night.

Blade stepped closer to Bertha. "I'm sorry," he told her.

"For what?"

"You were right. We never should have come in here in the dark. I should have listened to you."

"Apology accepted." She grinned. "I guess I ain't so dumb, after all."

"No one ever said you were."

"MUH-EET!"

"Let's get the hell out of here!" Hickok suggested.

Blade gazed at each of them. "It's imperative you get back to the SEAL. Let's go."

They ran, staying on University Avenue. From near and far came the distinct sounds of pursuit, as if invisible phantoms were all around them, circling them, waiting for the signal to pounce.

"This gives me the creeps," Hickok said. "I wish they'd do something!"

They did.

An overgrown hedgerow materialized, bordering University Avenue to their left. To their right, like a concrete and metal juggernaut, rose a five-story office building. Scraggly shrubbery lined the lawn between the road and the structure.

"Good spot for an ambush," Geronimo noted.

The Wacks swarmed on them out of the night, shrieking and hollering and babbling. Some carried bladed implements, others wielded clubs and boards, still others held large stones or bricks.

"MUH-EET!" thundered the incessant voice.

The first Wack, a grim, shapeless apparition in the black of night, reached the edge of University Avenue.

"Take this, sucker!" Bertha yelled a challenge, sighted, and fired. The crack of her Springfield was the catalyst, causing pandemonium to erupt.

The first Wack jerked backwards and tumbled to the ground. The remainder of the crazies screamed bloody murder.

The road in front abruptly became packed with indistinct forms.

Blade, in the lead, dropped to one knee, sweeping the Commando in an arc, the staccato burst clearing a path for them to proceed.

A brick struck Geronimo on the left shoulder. He spun, catching sight of a figure behind one of the bushes, and he let loose with the Browning. The Wack slammed into the earth.

"They're all over the place!" Hickok shouted. Stones and other hard objects were striking all over the road as the Wacks pelted them with everything they could lay their hands on. A pale face flashed at the top of the hedgerow, and Hickok snapped off a shot, the blast of the Henry followed by a piercing wail.

"Got ya'!"

"There's more here," Joshua said, as another group closed in on them from the rear. Instinctively, Joshua pumped the Smith and Wesson four times. The shadows screeched and dropped. Joshua looked down at his shotgun. Dear Father in heaven! What had he done? Killed again? He hesitated, not noticing he was falling behind the others, unaware of his danger until a sturdy hand gripped his shoulder and forcefully spun him around.

A Wack, a blurry image of torn clothes and thin

arms, raised a butcher knife above his head.

Joshua pulled the trigger.

The blast from the shotgun caught the Wack in the face, blowing it apart.

The others were fifteen yards ahead, grimly engaged in life-or-death combat, firing as fast as a target presented itself. They weren't aware that Joshua had dropped behind.

"Wait for me!" Joshua tried to make himself heard over the din. "Wait for me!"

A heavy chunk of concrete, hurtling out of the night, connected with the back of Joshua's head. Blood spurted as he sagged and dropped to his knees. A Wack ran up, raising a two-by-four.

Geronimo, concentrating on their right flank, thought he heard Joshua's voice. He whirled, catching a glimpse of a Wack about to bash in Joshua's head. The Browning blasted, catching the crazy in the chest, the force of impact propelling him backwards onto the road.

"Joshua!" Geronimo ran to Joshua's side and grabbed his right arm before he could fall to the pavement. "Get up! You have to get up!" Geronimo tugged, trying to raise Joshua to his feet, to get them moving.

A stone hit Geronimo's chin, stinging him, splitting the skin.

Joshua groaned.

"Get up!"

Their attackers, sensing a weak link in their defense, bore down on Geronimo and Joshua, wary now, hesitant to face the guns with over fifteen casualties already tallied in the first ninety seconds of the battle.

One of the Wacks approached and tossed a brick. The brick missed.

Geronimo's shot didn't.

Twenty-five yards ahead, Blade noticed some of the Wacks were dropping off. Why? he asked himself. He glanced around, freezing when he realized Geronimo and Joshua weren't with them any longer. Where? Where? He saw a commotion a ways behind, and caught the flash of the Browning as Geronimo fired again.

"Damn!"

Blade dodged a jagged piece of glass and reached Hickok's side. "You've got to get back to the SEAL! Don't wait for us!" With that, he ran back towards Geronimo and Joshua.

"What? What'd you say?" Hickok had missed Blade's words. He stopped, watching Blade run off. Where the blazes was he . . . Where were Joshua and Geronimo?

"Look out!"

Bertha stepped between Hickok and a charging Wack. She aimed for the head, feeling the recoil of the Springfield against her right shoulder at the same instant the crazy fell.

"Where are the others?" Hickok yelled.

Bertha suddenly realized they were alone. "Lordy! Let's get out of here!"

"We can't leave the others!" Hickok protested. He began to run back, managing only a few steps before they were cut off from their friends by a howling mob of zanies going after Blade.

"This way!" Bertha took hold of his sleeve. "The way in front is clear!"

Hickok fired four times at the group after Blade, downing four.

"Come on, White Meat! We got to get out of here!"

A tall crazy broke from the hedgerow, swinging a club. He lunged, bringing the club down, trying for Hickok's head, but missing and striking the barrel

97

of the Henry instead. The rifle clattered to the road and rolled out of sight.

Hickok ducked a second blow, drawing his right Python, putting the Wack away with a head shot.

Bertha tugged on Hickok's arm. There was a momentary lull around them, the crazies devoting their attention to Blade and the others. "We got to get out of here!"

"Not on your life! I won't leave my friends!"

The Commando and the Browning were still firing.

"You can't do them any good if you're dead! If we get out, we can come back and rescue 'em!"

Dozens of Wacks had surrounded Blade, Geronimo, and Joshua.

"I'm not leaving them!" Hickok declared stubbornly. He glanced around, searching for his Henry. "Where the blazes is my gun?" He bent over, trying to distinguish features in the dark, elated when he spotted the stock protruding from under a bush at the side of the road. "There it is!"

"Look out!"

This time Bertha's warning was too late. A short Wack jumping up from behind the bush, cackling insanely, holding a hammer. Quick as his reflexes were, Hickok managed one shot as the hammer smacked into his skull. Both men sprawled to the ground.

"Lordy, no!" Bertha crouched alongside Hickok, waiting for another attack. None came. She shook Hickok, trying to arouse him without success. Pressing her ear to his lips, she held her own breath and listened. He was breathing, barely.

The Python was on the pavement by his right hand.

Bertha replaced the Colt in its holster, tucked the Springfield under her left arm, and grabbed Hickok under her arms. She strained and pulled, dragging him behind the bush, hiding him.

The others were still fighting.

Bertha placed a protective hand on Hickok's head, flinching when a moist substance covered her hand. White Meat was hurt, and hurt bad. She couldn't leave him to help the rest, not now, not when he might die if she left. Cradling the Springfield in her arms, she leaned on Hickok's chest and probed the night, sweating it out, dreading the Wacks would find them.

No, sir.

The other three would have to fend for themselves.

If they could.

8

Miles away, in opposite directions, three factions heard the shots and marveled. There were few guns in the Twin Cities, and ammunition was scarce. No one would use ammo as indiscriminately as it was being used in the battle they were hearing.

In camp one, a handsome, muscular man with brown hair and blue eyes turned to one of his men. "I want six men ready to go as soon as possible. This bears investigating."

"Right away, Z."

In camp two, an obese, bald blob of a man slapped a confederate on the cheek. "Send some patrols out. Find out what the hell is going on!"

"You got it, Maggot!"

In camp three, the farthest away, a short, gray-haired man with penetrating green eyes, mused aloud. "Earlier we heard that one brief burst of gunfire, and now it sounds as if a veritable war is being waged. Ordinarily, we should refrain from entering that hell hole at night, but this case is an exception. Our curiosity must be satisfied. Send out a patrol. Instruct them to ascertain the source of firing."

"At once, brother," responded the second in command. "Your will be done."

9

He found her leaning against a tree, gazing sadly up at the heavens. The light from his torch revealed the frown on her face.

"I enjoy watching the stars too," he said, announcing his presence. "Communing outdoors accentuates the experience."

She started, apparently unaware of his arrival until he spoke. "I'm sorry," she apologized. "I was preoccupied. I didn't hear you come up. What did you say?"

"It's not important." He sighed, his frail shoulders sagging. "You miss him terribly, don't you, Jenny?"

"Of course. Don't you, Plato? You two are very close."

"He's like the son I never fathered," Plato admitted. "I wish I had never sent the Alpha Triad out."

Jenny put her arm around him. "Don't fret. Your regret is uncalled for. You had to do what's best for the entire Family."

"That's what I constantly tell myself," Plato said.

"Small consolation if anything should happen to any of them."

"The Spirit will guide them," Jenny assured him, trying to assuage his emotional misery.

"I know."

"And the Alpha Triad is comprised of the best Warriors in the Family. You've told me so yourself. Blade, Hickok, and Geronimo can take care of themselves in a pinch. You don't need to worry about them."

Plato nodded. No matter how many times someone tried to comfort him, he couldn't shake a nagging feeling of foreboding. Was it for the Alpha Triad or the Family? he wondered. He silently prayed Blade would return soon. His informant had told him the power-monger, the Family malcontent, was becoming more vocal in his expressions of dissatisfaction with the Family system. He desperately needed Blade. If words failed to rectify the situation and appease the errant rebel, Blade might well be the one man who could successfully prevent a bloody revolution.

"Are you okay?" Jenny asked him. "You look tired, too tired."

"I'm fine," Plato lied. "I've never felt better."

"I wonder what Blade's doing right now?" Jenny's concern surfaced again.

"I'm certain he's having a good night's rest," Plato told her. "Exactly as you should be doing. It's getting a bit chilly. Permit me to walk you back."

"All right," Jenny reluctantly agreed. "I suppose I could use some sleep."

"I bet Blade's dreaming about you right this minute." Plato smiled reassuringly.

"I bet you're right."

10

Blade savagely rammed the stock of the Commando into the stomach of a Wack who'd grabbed him from behind. As the crazy doubled over, Blade spun, firing, nearly cutting his attacker in half at the waist.

A stone dropped down from the darkness, catching Blade on the left side, bruising his ribs.

"We've got to get out of here!" Geronimo shouted.

Another Wack, heedless of personal risk, came at them from the right.

Geronimo held the Browning braced against his right hip and fired.

"You got him!" Blade exulted.

Amazingly, the assault ceased.

"Where'd they go?" Geronimo asked, searching, believing the respite might be a deliberate ruse.

"Maybe to regroup," Blade suggested. "They've lost a lot already."

"Over two dozen," Geronimo guessed. "I can't believe they just keep coming."

Blade checked the magazine in his Commando. "If

they do keep coming, I'm going to run out of ammunition. We've got to get back to the SEAL. We've plenty of ammo there."

"Where's Hickok and Bertha?" Geronimo anxiously inquired.

"I told them to get back to the transport," Blade answered. "They must have made it."

"I hope so."

"How's Joshua?"

Joshua was still on his knees, pressing his left hand against the gash in the back of his head. His long hair was matted with dried blood. "I'm able to stand," Joshua replied for himself. He grit his teeth and managed to heave erect, weaving.

"Take it easy," Geronimo admonished him. "We're right here. We'll help you."

"Sorry to be such a burden."

"You're no burden," Blade stated. "It looks like they've gone, so we can get out of here."

From the blackness to their left bellowed the familiar refrain: "MUH-EET! MUH-EET!"

"Damn!" Blade crouched, waiting, knowing the Wacks weren't through with them.

"Let's go!" Geronimo urged, leading the way.

The Wacks literally poured from the darkness, filling the road in front of them.

"They're trying to block our retreat!" Geronimo yelled.

Blade, furious, fired, holding the trigger down, unleashing a lethal barrage into the writhing mass of hostility in their path.

It wasn't enough.

"Now!" a male voice screamed, and all the Wacks there let fly with whatever they were holding in their hands.

There was nowhere to take cover.

Blade, Geronimo, and Joshua futilely attempted

to shield their bodies from the downpour of stones, bricks, glass, metal, and other objects. They twitched and convulsed as they were pelted, lancing agony piercing their limbs and torsos.

The Wacks howled, still tossing their arsenal.

Blade gave Geronimo a slight shove. "Get the hell out of here!"

"I won't leave you," Geronimo snapped defiantly.

"Think of Joshua," Blade reminded him. "Head east. I'll catch up in a bit. You'll need me to cover for you. We're too exposed on this avenue. I'll hold them off, then join you."

"I don't know . . ."

Joshua moaned, almost collapsing.

Geronimo caught him with his left arm.

"Go!" Blade ordered. "This is no time to argue!"

Geronimo grimly nodded. He supported Joshua, leading him from the road, hurrying to find any cover, any defensible position.

Blade watched them go, aware the deluge had stopped. Geronimo and Joshua disappeared, and he was totally alone. He turned his attention to the Wacks, startled to discover they had vanished too.

Damn!

Where were they? Planning another attack? Bertha had said the Wacks were crazy. How crazy? What were the limits of their mental capacities? Could they carry out a complicated method of attack?

A solitary rock hurtled from his left, missing.

Annoyed, Blade fired a short burst in the direction the projectile had originated from. He was rewarded by a shriek of pain.

Serves the bastards right!

Slowly, alertly, Blade backed away, intent on following Geronimo and Joshua, afraid they would get too great a start and be impossible to locate in the dark.

A shadow ran at him from the murky gloom, a female Wack with a knife clutched in her left hand.

Blade remorselessly mowed her down.

"MUH-EET!"

Where was the bozo with the monosyllabic vocabulary?

Blade reached the eastern edge of University Avenue, hesitating, hoping he could lose the Wacks in the nocturnal terrain. He doubted it, though. Considering their accuracy, the crazies must possess exceptional night vision. Possibly, after decades of hunting and foraging after dark, their eyes were adjusted to the lack of light.

The snap of a twig apprised him of the danger an instant before a zany jumped at him with a pitchfork.

Blade rolled, the rusted prongs of the pitchfork lancing by his head. He fired from the prone position, on his back, the heavy slugs ripping the Wack from the crotch to his neck.

"MUH-EET!"

Blade crouched, debating. It was definitely time to haul butt and catch up with Geronimo and Joshua. He ran, hunched over, trying to make his body as small a target as he could. Bushes and weeds choked the lawn he was crossing. A tree rose in front of him and he dodged the trunk, hearing a scraping above him as he passed under the branches.

Damn!

The Wack pounced on his back, bearing them both to the grass, iron fingers closing around his throat, the Commando useless, pinned under his chest.

Damn!

Blade tried to rise, but the crazy on top of him was endowed with the abnormal strength of madness.

"Want the legs!" the Wack babbled.

The legs?

"Legs taste good!" the Wack cackled. "Legs taste good!"

Blade groped for the dagger on his left wrist, finding the handle, drawing the knife from its sheath and sweeping it back and up.

"Uuuurrk!" The Wack, shocked, released the death grip.

Blade shoved upward, dislodging his assailant. He clutched the Commando, whirled, and fired. The crazy flopped and tossed as the bullets ravaged his body.

Definitely time to get the hell out of here!

The next blackened form was already coming at him from the other side of the tree.

Blade pressed the trigger as the Wack swung a tire iron, expecting the chattering blast would decimate the lunatic.

The Commando jammed.

Blade brought the Carbine up, blocking the iron. He brutally jabbed the stock into the Wack's throat, crushing the windpipe.

"MUH-EET!"

Blade threw caution to the winds and ran, heedless of the risk and the undergrowth impeding his progress. He considered dropping the Commando, but the gun was too valuable to lose. Holding the useless Carbine in his left hand, he drew a Vega with his right.

Something swished through the air and imbedded itself in Blade's left thigh. He stumbled and went down, intense agony racking his entire leg.

What the . . . ?

Blade probed, his fingers contacting a thin shaft

sticking into his thigh. An arrow! He'd been shot with a damn arrow! The Spirit help him!

The brush around him came alive with soft rustlings and indistinct whisperings.

The Wacks were coming for him!

Blade angrily gripped the shaft with both hands and wrenched the arrow free. Moist blood flowed freely over his thigh.

The nearest shrub parted and someone stepped into view.

Blade grabbed the Vega and fired three times.

Whoever it was fell out of sight.

Blade shuffled forward, determined to escape. There was still a chance he could shake his pursuers. He had to find Geronimo and Joshua! He had to!

"MUH-EET!" came from behind him, the basso bellow of the town crier.

The weeds thinned out, ending in a paved square that once had served as a parking lot for fifty automobiles.

Blade paused, wavering over the peril of exposing himself in the open. But then what choice did he have? Pressing his left hand on the arrow wound to suppress the flow of blood, he hobbled across the tarmac, the hairs on the back of his neck tingling from a sense of anticipated menace.

Another arrow zinged by his right shoulder.

Blade twisted, catching a glimpse of a form standing near the pavement. The bowman notching another shaft. Blade raised the Vega, carefully sighted, and fired. The boom of the gun and the scream of the Wack were instantaneous.

As Hickok would say, Got ya!

Blade limped on, heading for the far side of the parking lot. There appeared to be dense brush and trees ahead, and if he could reach that cover, he could elude the crazies on his heels.

The pounding of feet on the tarmac behind him reached his ears.

Blade glanced back over his shoulder.

Four Wacks had burst from the weeds, intent on catching him before he could attain the other side.

Blade knew they'd be on him before he could fire twice. This was no time for the gun. He smiled grimly. This situation called for dirty infighting, his specialty. He quickly holstered the Vega and drew his two Bowies, reassured by the feel of the heavy handles in his hands. Let them come!

They did.

The first attacker came at him with an upraised shovel, the tool held over his head. Blade jumped in close, before the Wack could swing, and slashed the Bowie in his right hand across the zany's left wrist.

The Wack's left hand dropped to the ground, the man frozen in his tracks, horrified, watching the hand flap for a few seconds as the fingers twitched.

"Clorg!" the crazy shouted, terrified, holding the stump up to his face and gaping as blood spurted in every direction. "Clorg!"

Blade was already in motion, avoiding the first stab of the second assailant, who leaped at him with a knife. A flash of pale flesh revealed Blade's target, and he buried his left Bowie in the man's neck. To the hilt. He fiercely twisted the blade, then yanked the Bowie clear.

The third Wack came in fast and low, diving for Blade's legs.

Blade cried out as the attacker collided with his injured left leg, and he went down, trying to orient his position in relation to the two Wacks still capable of fighting. He lashed with his right foot and caught the man who'd tackled him in the face, crushing the Wack's nose.

Where was the fourth one? Blade struggled to rise. There had been one more when . . .

11

"Where are the others?"

"Be quiet."

"But we can't desert the others!"

"We'll find them. You've got to stay silent, Joshua."

"It's so hard for me to think," Joshua complained, his head reeling.

"You've been hurt," Geronimo stated. "You need rest. I don't know how bad your injury is."

Geronimo, supporting Joshua with his brawny left arm, led him deeper into the trees they had discovered on the other end of the wide paved area.

"I don't think I can stay awake," Joshua mumbled sleepily.

"Just for a little bit more," Geronimo urged him.

"I'll try," Joshua feebly promised.

Geronimo glanced back, extremely concerned. Blade should have caught up with them by now. Had he been killed or captured? What did the Wacks do with their victims? Bertha had told them the Wacks ate other people. Great Spirit! How disgusting!

"I can't go on," Joshua muttered drowsily. "I'm sorry, 'ronimo."

Joshua passed out.

Geronimo lowered Joshua to the grass. They were in a small space between two large trees. The two trunks would provide some shelter and seclusion. Geronimo flattened and pressed his right ear against the ground.

Footsteps. Coming their way!

Geronimo squatted, holding the Browning. He wasn't about to leave Joshua. If the Wacks found them, he would go down as a Warrior should. He gazed at Joshua. Funny. Joshua wasn't a Warrior, but he'd performed superbly back on University Avenue, despite his pacifist, spiritual convictions.

Someone grunted.

Geronimo tensed, ready.

"Any sign of them?" a voice fifteen yards away asked.

"Nope," replied another.

"Clorg not be happy," said a third.

"Clorg will be happy with one we got."

"Not much food," complained the second man.

"But is big one."

"Not much food," the second man insisted. "Maybe two feeds if that."

"We find more tonight."

"Let's go back."

"Okay."

"Say, Miffle?"

"Yes?"

"Seen my finger? I dropped it."

"Your own fault," Miffle said. "Should not carry with."

"Didn't mean to cut it off," apologized the Wack. "Was skinning skunk."

"We knew."

"Let's get big man back to Fant."

All three laughed.

The voices faded.

Geronimo, puzzled, stood. They hadn't made much sense, but he did gather they had captured a "big man." Had to be Blade. What should he do now? Stay with Joshua or go aid Blade? His mind whirled. If he stayed here, the Wacks would cart Blade off to wherever they lived and eat him. But, if he left Joshua to follow the Wacks, something might find Joshua in the dark and finish him off. There was no telling how long it might be before he had an opportunity to free Blade, even if he did trail the Wacks.

Great Spirit, preserve him!

Geronimo sat, cross-legged, and moodily contemplated their predicament. They were separated. They were cut off from the SEAL. They were in hostile territory with one Warrior a prisoner and Joshua hurt. Where were Hickok and Bertha?

Joshua moaned in his sleep.

Geronimo placed his right hand on Joshua's forehead. Just what they needed! Joshua had a fever.

Geronimo made up his mind. He would stay with Joshua until morning, tend to his wound, leave him the Browning, and track the Wacks to where they were holding Blade. He'd rather take the Browning, but the Smith and Wesson was gone, probably dropped by Joshua when he was hit on the head.

His thoughts took a morbid turn. What if they never returned? What would the Family do? Send out more Warriors to find them, although Plato had promised not to? What if the Wacks ate Blade before he got there? What if Hickok and Bertha were dead? He stared up at the stars, praying for the sun.

113

12

The bright light on her eyelids woke her up.

Bertha involuntarily started, pushing herself up from Hickok's chest, blinking rapidly, trying to adjust her eyes to the morning sun.

She must have dozed off!

That thought immediately woke her up. What was the matter with her, falling asleep in no-man's-land? Was she as crazy as the Wacks? To her credit, she had managed to fight off fatigue until an hour before sunrise, succumbing because her system was emotionally overwrought and she was extremely fatigued. She had been unable to sleep soundly since leaving the Home.

Bertha stared at Hickok. He was breathing, his chest rising and falling in a regular rhythm. Dried blood caked the left side of his head, shading his blond hair a dull brown. There was a circular indentation in the center. She gently raised the hair and intently examined the wound. It didn't appear to be deep, but she worried nonetheless, dreading he might have sustained brain damage. She wouldn't know until she revived him. And the sooner, the better.

Birds were chirping in nearby trees.

A good sign. If danger was present, the singing birds would fall silent.

Bertha rose, her legs stiff, clutching the Springfield. She cautiously stepped around in front of the bush and onto University Avenue. Bodies of Wacks were scattered along the road and on both sides. Bad news. Bodies would attract vermin, rats and dogs and worse. She had to get Hickok on his feet and get him back to the SEAL, or at least to a safe hiding place. Water was what she needed.

A crow flew in from the south, circling over the bodies, cawing its find to its brothers and sisters.

Bertha walked north on University Avenue, searching for water, for anything she could use to revivify Hickok. Three blocks passed and she stopped, loath to go any further, to stray too far from the gunman.

To her left stood a decrepit office building, two stories high. The windows were busted, the doors long gone. Before the war, a fountain had delighted passersby with a ten-foot-high jet of spray. Now the fountain basin served as a large catch bowl for rainwater.

Bertha ran to the basin and dropped to her knees. This was just what she needed, but how would she carry the water back to Hickok? She glanced around, frowning, disappointed, because there was nothing she could use.

"Planning to take a bath, Bertha?"

Bertha spun, seeing she was covered by a man with a rifle and two other men with bows, the arrows notched and aimed at her. She recognized the six men surrounding her.

"Say, there, bro! How does it go?"

"Don't give me any jive, honey," the man with the rifle said. "Stand up. Real slow."

Bertha did as she was told. "What's the matter with you, Tommy? Is this any way to treat your old friend Bertha?"

Tommy, like the others, was dressed in shabby, grungy clothes. His black hair was long, past his shoulders, and he sported a beard.

"Old friend Bertha?" Tommy repeated, his finger on the trigger. "We all thought you was dead. We haven't heard from you in weeks. Z took it real hard. He thought you'd been wasted by the Watchers or the Uglies."

"And here I am." Bertha beamed. "Alive and kickin'!" She could sense their suspicion, their wariness, and she couldn't blame them. She'd feel the same way if the situation were reversed.

"Very strange," Tommy stated. "Here we all think you're dead and gone, and look at you! New clothes! A beaut of a gun! And you're lookin' healthy and well fed! Someone's taking good care of you, aren't they, babe?"

"I don't have time to talk right now." Bertha took a step toward them.

Tommy jerked the stock to his shoulder. "Not one more step, Bertha! I'm warning you."

Bertha thought of Hickok, alone and defenseless, needing her. "I ain't got time to explain," she said impatiently.

"Boys," Tommy told the others, "if she takes another step, put an arrow into her."

"Tommy! It's me, Bertha!" She angrily stamped her right foot. "What the hell is the matter with you?"

"The only reason you ain't already dead," Tommy informed her, "is because we was friends, once."

"Tommy . . ."

"Don't press it!" he warned her. "Just put that gun on the ground. We're takin' you back to Z. There's a lot of questions he's gonna want to ask you, sweet cheeks."

"Maybe she's gone back to the Porns," one of the other men suggested.

Tommy nodded slowly. "I done thought of that. Which is why we treat her like we would any enemy . . . or traitor!"

"I ain't no traitor!" Bertha snapped.

"Oh? How do we know that?"

"Tommy, listen to me . . ."

"Not now. We ain't got the time. We heard a lot of shooting last night and came for a look-see. The Horns and the Porns might do the same. We're headin' back, and we're takin' you with us."

"I can't go with you."

"You ain't got much choice, honey."

Bertha weighed the odds. They weren't good. If she tried to buck them, they'd get her before she could fire a shot.

"I don't like the way she's just standing there," another Nomad said.

"Let's get the hell out of here," added yet another.

"You heard them," Tommy said to Bertha. "I'm real sorry, babe, we got to treat you this way. You understand, don't you?"

"I do," she agreed. "But you've got to let me explain . . ."

"Not now. Tell it to Z. Drop the gun."

"Tommy, listen." Bertha took a step towards him.

One of the bowmen let fly.

"No!" Tommy shouted at the same instant.

In what seemed like slow motion, Bertha watched the brown shaft come at her, the feathers spinning as the arrow covered the fifteen yards between the bowman and her. The point, a nail imbedded in the top of the shaft with the flattened head removed and filed to a sharp edge, glistened in the sunlight, coming closer and closer and . . .

The arrow slammed into Bertha's body, slicing into her above her right breast, penetrating, the impact twisting her to the side, stunning her.

"Damn!" Tommy fumed. "She wasn't going to hurt us!"

"But you said to shoot if she came at you," the bowman protested.

Bertha recognized the man who had fired. Vint. He always was an asshole!

Tommy ran up to her. "Bertha! You okay?"

The shock was spreading, numbing her. She sagged, her legs weakening.

Tommy caught her. "Damn! Look at all that blood!"

Bertha's mind was spinning. She vainly attempted to focus. "Tommy . . ."

"I'm here. We'll get you back and take care of you."

"No. No," she said weakly. "Listen. Got to help . . ."

"We'll help you," he assured her.

"No. Not me. Help him. Got to help him." Her voice was a whisper.

"Help who?"

"Help . . . him. Hurt. Help White Mea . . ." She went limp in his arms.

"She's out," one of the Nomads announced.

"I can see that!" Tommy spat.

"Do you really think she went over to the Porns?" Vint asked.

"After what Maggot did to her?" Tommy shook his head. "Not likely. This poor girl has the worst luck of anyone I've ever seen!"

"I'm sorry I hurt her," Vint apologized. "I always liked her. I was just doing what you told me."

"Yeah." Tommy sadly stared at Bertha. "Me and my big mouth. Let's get out of here! She needs help."

"What about the other one she mentioned?" another Nomad brought up.

"Who knows?"

"Maybe someone was with her. Maybe he's around here somewhere, and needs help."

"If he does," Tommy said, "it's too bad for him. We can't take the time to look all over the place. Whoever she was tryin' to tell us about is all on his own."

13

Geronimo was greatly relieved when dawn finally broke. He stood and stretched. Joshua was still unconscious, and rest was best for him in his condition. Geronimo yawned. He could use some sleep himself. He'd give Joshua another hour, then wake him, minister to the injury, and begin tracking the Wacks.

An idea occurred to him.

If Joshua had dropped the Smith and Wesson somewhere between their hiding place and University Avenue, he might be able to find it and leave it with Joshua. That way, he could take the Browning with him. He'd need the firepower if he caught up with the Wacks. If? If he didn't, Blade was dead.

Joshua still had the leather pouch containing the Ruger Redhawk draped over his right shoulder. He'd need more than that, if left alone. Joshua wasn't experienced with guns, and the shotgun would serve him in better stead.

Geronimo crouched and headed for the road, keeping low, moving rapidly from cover to cover, pausing to listen and look at the slightest noise. He reached a parking lot and froze.

Two bodies lay in the center of the tarmac, another one at the edge of the weeds on the far side.

Blade?

Geronimo sped across the parking lot, into the brush on the other side. He almost tripped over another dead Wack, and further on found two more lying under a large tree. If the Wacks had indeed captured Blade, it had cost them dearly. He smiled, feeling strangely assured by the dead Wacks. The only Warrior in the Family capable of equaling Blade's aptitude for killing was Hickok, and possibly Rikki-Tikki-Tavi, but when Blade lost his temper, not even the gunman could match his primal fury.

He reached University Avenue, discovering a lifeless Wack glaring up at the blue sky, a pitchfork nearby. And at the verge of the road, almost obscured by thick weeds, the Smith and Wesson. He was stooping to pick it up when he heard the tittering giggle. Automatically, he flattened and rolled to his right, sighting down the Browning, searching for the source of the laugh.

She was standing in the open, about ten yards west of University Avenue, holding her bloody left arm pressed against her side. Torn, filthy rags hung from her emaciated form. All visible skin was covered with dirt and her hair was plastered with dried mud. She was smiling, exposing gaps where her front teeth once were.

Geronimo warily rose, expecting other Wacks to come charging at him any moment.

None came.

The girl jumped up and down and cackled.

"Hello," Geronimo ventured, trying to engage her in conversation. "Who are you?"

121

She spun completely around, pointed at him with her right hand, and cackled harder.

What was the matter with her? Besides the obvious?

"My name is Geronimo," he offered hopefully. "What's yours?"

The girl shook her head.

How old was she? Eighteen? Twenty at the most.

"Can I help you?" Geronimo slowly stepped towards her. Maybe, if he could establish a friendship, gain her trust, she would lead him to where the Wacks were holding Blade.

She shyly lowered her eyes and backed away.

"Don't!" he called out. "Please, don't!"

The girl turned and began running off.

What should he do now? If he went after her, Joshua would be left unattended until he returned, vulnerable to attack. On the other hand, if he didn't pursue the girl, he'd lose a golden opportunity to find the Wacks' lair. He could compromise, follow her as far as feasible, then return to Joshua.

Geronimo ran after her.

The Wack fled like a panicked gazelle, darting between trees and bushes with amazing grace and timing.

Geronimo was hard pressed to keep her in sight.

She followed a narrow green belt between two cluster of buildings, sure of herself, as if she knew where she was going and had a definite destination in mind.

Geronimo tried in vain to gain on her.

The Wack reached a road, paused to glance back and insure she was still being followed, then she ran across the road and into a narrow alley separating two tall structures.

Geronimo stopped at the alley entrance. The alley was dim, the ten-story buildings diminishing the sunlight reaching into it. Piles and piles of debris and garbage littered both sides of the alley, leaving only a cramped, sinuous path threading towards the dark recess of the alley's interior.

The setup was unsettling.

Geronimo suspected a trap, but in those limited confines any attackers would be compelled to attack him one at a time, and he'd easily be able to defend himself with the Browning. It couldn't hurt to follow the alley for a short distance and see where it led. There seemed to be a high wall at the far end, perhaps fifty yards away.

Despite warnings from his better judgment, Geronimo entered the alley, the stench overpowering, his moccasins sinking an inch into a slimy muck with every step he took. A lot of garbage he passed was relatively fresh, deposited recently. By the Wacks? He noticed a considerable number of bones, all apparently from animals, a white contrast to the dark alley.

Where had the girl gone?

Geronimo proceeded for thirty yards into the alley, then hesitated. This was dumb. He wasn't getting any closer to Blade, and Joshua was unprotected in their hiding place. Squatting, he studied the tracks. A number of people had passed this way in the past eight to twelve hours. The mire was a maze of footprints. Odd. Where would they all be going? Well, he didn't have the time to find out. He'd left Joshua alone too long as it was. He stood, prepared to leave.

"Want to play dolls with me?"

The girl was ten yards from him, swaying, grinning, twirling her bangs with her right hand.

"What?" he asked, not sure he'd heard correctly.

"Fant show you his toes."

There was that peculiar name again. "Who is

123

Fant?'' he inquired.

She laughed insanely. "Dummy! Dummy! Dummy! Fant not who, not you or me. Don't you see?''

He didn't see. "Will you run away if I come closer?''

She demurely shook her head.

"You'll stay?''

"Me stay.''

Geronimo edged forward. The girl was as good as her word, staying exactly where she was. Considering her earlier flight, this behavior was strangely ominous. Why would she suddenly pop out of nowhere, acting friendly, actually waiting for him to approach? If she was as crazy as she appeared, no explanation was necessary. But if a shred of sanity remained, then this could well be a ruse designed to lead him into an ambush. He glanced up.

Just in time to save his life.

Perched on top of the garbage to his right, a knife held ready in the left hand, was a male Wack. Even as Geronimo saw him, he screeched and launched himself straight down.

Geronimo already had the Browning tilted up at an angle. He shifted, pulling the trigger, the blast catching the Wack in the chest and deflecting his leap to one side. The Wack crashed into the pile of debris, his head and shoulder disappearing from view.

The girl screamed and ran.

"Wait!'' Geronimo called after her. "Don't go!'' He loped in pursuit, surprised when she abruptly wheeled, laughing again, laughing and pointing at the ground at his feet. What in the world . . .

His feet gave out from under him, and he was dropping down into a hole in the ground. He tried to grab the edge of the hole, gripping the metal rim with his right hand, his left hand still holding the Browning and pinned between his body and the opening. For the moment, he was caught, unable to climb out and slowly slipping down.

Someone was standing over him, cackling.

Geronimo tried to strengthen his hold and failed, the effort costing him several inches. He was now dangling up to his chest.

"Dummy! Dummy! Dummy!" the girl taunted him.

"Help me! Please!" He tried to find something to support his suspended feet, but nothing was in reach.

"Dummy! Dummy! Dummy!"

He was continuing to slip.

"Say hi to Teeth," the girl said, smiling.

Teeth?

Geronimo was in to his shoulders and the Browning was loose in his hand. He had one chance. If he could grab the edge with his left hand, he would be able to pull himself up. But, to do that, he had to let go of the Browning. There wasn't any choice.

The girl leaned over and patted him on the head. "Bye-bye."

He released the Browning and brought his left hand up, managing to get a hold on the rim before he could plummet into the depths below. Without the Browning between his body and the rim, he would fall like a stone. His swinging feet touched a surface, a ledge or something similar he could use for support, and he braced himself for the heave to the surface.

"Not nice," the girl said gravely. "Not nice."

What the hell was she babbling about?

"Not nice," she repeated, stepping closer, drawing her right foot back.

"Wait . . ." he tried to protest.

125

She kicked him in the head, above his right ear.

Reeling, Geronimo frantically tried to clamber out of the manhole.

She kicked him again.

His hold was fading.

And again.

He couldn't seem to concentrate and his legs were sagging.

Again.

Geronimo felt his hands release their grip, and he plunged out of sight.

The girl waved at the black hole.

"Bye-bye!"

14

He had the impression his entire universe was comprised of sheer pain, and he didn't want to open his eyes to face a cosmos bent on torturing him. Memories filtered through his brain. The trip to the Twin Cities. Bertha. The Wacks. The Wacks! He remembered their attack, and the one with the hammer, and he flinched and opened his eyes, wishing he hadn't as waves of agony rippled along his nervous system.

Blast!

"Well, well, well," said a deep voice. "Look who's finally woke up!"

"I was sure he wasn't gonna make it," snapped a squeaky voice.

"Pay up."

"I ain't got it."

"You best have it."

Hickok rose on his elbows. He was lying on a cot in a small room, sunlight streaming in through a shattered window. Two men were in the room with him, one standing on either side of the only door.

"I'll get it," said the small man on the right, a

man with tiny eyes and a small nose, wearing faded jeans and a torn blue shirt.

"A bet is a bet," said the big man to the left of the door. "You bet six rounds he wasn't gonna come out of it, and you were wrong. I'd best have my ammo by the end of the week." This one wore only jeans, his torso bare and bulging with power, his black skin blending with the shadows in his corner. He was holding a Winchester in his left hand, a 30-30.

"You'll get it, Bear," reiterated the other. "I always make good." He had a revolver strapped around his waist, a Taurus Model 86 in the holster on his left hip.

"I know you do, Rat."

"Excuse me, gentlemen," Hickok blithely interrupted. "Could I bother you for a drink? My throat is awful dry."

"Is it, now?" Rat grinned. "You'll get a drink when we're damn ready to give you one and not before."

"You know, ugly," Hickok said coldly, "if I was feeling any stronger, I'd get up out of this cot and stuff your face up your ass. Who knows? The view might improve your disposition."

Rat clenched his fists and came at Hickok.

"Cool it, Rat," the one called Bear warned.

"You heard what he said to me!" Rat exploded, stopping.

"I heard." Bear laughed.

Rat reddened. "No one talks like that to me and lives!"

"Our orders are to keep him alive," Bear said.

Rat glared at Hickok, his fists opening and closing. "I'll get my chance," he stated. "Sooner or later."

"I don't think I've ever been this scared in my life," Hickok grinned.

Rat reluctantly backed to the door.

"You believe in living dangerously, don't you?" Bear asked Hickok.

"Is there any other way?"

Bear walked over to the cot. "How you feeling?"

"Plumb tuckered out," Hickok admitted. "I take it I'm your prisoner?"

"You got that right."

"And who are you guys? Horns?"

This time it was Rat who laughed. "Did you hear that? He thinks we're Horns? What an idiot!"

"Which proves that Maggot was right, as usual," Bear said. "This one ain't from the Twins."

"Where you from?" Rat demanded.

"Wouldn't you like to know?" Hickok retorted.

"We'll find out," Rat promised. "Sooner or later."

Hickok took stock of his weapons. The Henry and the Pythons were gone, but he could feel the Derringer on his right wrist and the C.O.P. .357 Magnum strapped to his left leg, above the ankle. Both guns were hidden by his buckskins. Good. He wasn't defenseless.

"How'd I get here?" Hickok asked them.

"We sent a patrol out after hearing a lot of shooting the night before last," Bear answered. "They found you out cold."

Hickok sat up. "You mean I've been here a day and a half?" he asked incredulously.

"Sure have. The patrol was checkin' bodies on University Avenue when they found you still alive. Had a nasty bump on the head. They couldn't figure out what you were. You sure weren't no Wack, and you weren't dressed like a Horn, and you ain't one of us. They decided to bring you back to Maggot."

"Who's Maggot?"

Rat snickered. "You'll meet him soon enough."

"Maggot's our main man," Bear replied.

"Your boss?"

"Yeah. He calls the shots."

Hickok had noticed a trend. "You're called Bear," he said to the black, "and ugly over there is called Rat, and now you tell me your leader is someone called Maggot. What's with the names? Why are they all animal or insect names?"

"Sharp one, ain't you?" Bear complimented him. "The names are Maggot's idea. He's got this book all about wild creatures, and he gets a kick out of namin' us according to the book. He says he tries to pick a name that fits the person."

"Rat sure fits him." Hickok indicated Rat. "But I can't imagine anyone wanting to call himself Maggot."

"You'll understand, soon enough," Bear said slowly. "What's your name, anyhow?"

"Hickok." He extended his right hand.

Bear stared at the hand for a few awkward seconds, evidently surprised it had been offered. Finally, he shook with a firm, strong grip.

"Pleased to meet you, Bear," Hickok said. "Any chance of me getting some food? I could eat a . . . bear." He grinned.

So did the black. "We'll get you something."

"But Maggot said we was to take him as soon as he woke up," whined Rat in protest.

"Some food won't hurt," Bear stated harshly. "Go get some."

"Why me?"

Bear pivoted, fixing his eyes on Rat. "Because I told you to, that's why."

Rat reached for the door handle.

"And keep your mouth shut," Bear warned.

Rat left.

"I take it you guys are Porns?" Hickok said.

Bear nodded. "You know an awful lot about the

Twins. Where are you from, Hickok?"

"Sorry, Bear, but I think I best keep that information to myself."

Bear shrugged. "Where'd you learn so much about the Twins, about the Horns and Porns and such?"

"From a friend."

"This friend have a name?"

"Guess it can't hurt." Hickok reflected a moment. "You might even know her. She mentioned she was once a Porn. Her name is Bertha."

Bear's mouth dropped at the sound of her name. He crouched next to the cot, studying Hickok's face. "Bertha?"

"Yeah. You know her then?"

Bear nodded. "We were friends," he said ruefully, "before she went over to the Nomads."

"Why'd she switch?"

Bear frowned. "Didn't she tell you? She went over because of Maggot."

"Maggot?"

"Yeah. He thinks he can have any woman he wants, any time he wants. He wanted Bertha, and she told him to go screw himself."

"Sounds like our girl."

"Yeah." Bear smiled. "She's a scrapper! But Maggot didn't take to the idea of being told no. He had her tortured."

"Tortured? How?"

Bear averted his eyes, the memory filling him with a sense of shame. "Maggot had her arms tied over her head, and she was dangled in the pit. He thought it would break her."

"What's the pit?"

Bear shuddered. "Maggot's special place for those he don't like. The pit connects to tunnels, and when someone is thrown in the pit, the rats pour out of the tunnels and eat the poor son of a bitch alive!'' Bear paused, wiping his brow with his hand.

"He did that to her?"

Bear swallowed. "Yeah, but instead of throwin' her in, Maggot put a beam across the top of the pit and hung her from it so she was just out of the rat's reach. Some of the bigger rats, though, could get her legs if they jumped real hard. Maggot kept her there for three days, until she got away somehow. The next we heard, she'd joined the Nomads."

"How'd she get away?"

"Don't rightly know," Bear responded. "Maggot thinks someone helped her escape."

"Who would do that?" Hickok asked, smiling.

Bear didn't notice the smile. "Beats me. If Maggot ever finds out who it is, they're dead."

"Thanks for telling me," Hickok said. "It sure explains a couple of things about Bertha."

"You say you're friends?"

"Yep."

"Where is she now?"

"I wish I knew," Hickok said sadly. "The last I knew, she was with me, fighting the Wacks. I don't know where she is now."

Bear glanced at the closed door, then at Hickok., "Listen, bro, and listen good! Your life ain't worth dirt here. Maggot is goin' to kill you. It's only a matter of when. Don't let him convince you otherwise. He will kill you!"

"Real hospitable to strangers in these parts," Hickok muttered. "Are all the Porns so ruthless?"

"No. There's a lot who don't like the way things is done."

"Then why don't they do something about it?" Hickok asked.

"Like what?"

"Like kill Maggot and take over?"

Bear's eyes widened fearfully. "Shut your mouth, honky! You got to keep thoughts like that to yourself!"

"Why don't they?" Hickok insisted.

Bear checked the door again. "Because Maggot's men got all the guns, and no one is allowed to get close to Maggot with a weapon. Even if Maggot were killed, there's no tellin' who would take over the Porns. Might be someone worse."

Hickok was digesting that bit of information when the door opened and Rat entered, bearing a tray of food.

Bear quickly stood.

"I got the food," Rat announced. "And I ran into someone at the food pots. He wanted to come back with me."

Hickok didn't like the way Rat's eyes were gleaming.

"Who?" Bear asked.

"Me," said a growling voice, and another man filled the doorway, a huge, obese mass of a man, bald on top, wearing baggy pants and a shirt sewn together from numerous other garments. Sweat covered his face, beads of moisture dripping from his thick double chin. He was carrying the Henry, and the two Pythons were tucked into his waistband.

Bear backed away several steps. "Maggot!"

"You were expecting Reverend Paul?" Maggot rumbled.

Rat laughed, reaching the cot and handing the tray to an aching Hickok. The meal consisted of soup and a glass of water.

Maggot lumbered up to the cot. Behind him, four other men, armed to the teeth, came into the room.

Maggot's bodyguard, Hickok reflected. He took a sip of the tepid water, feigning indifference to

Maggot's presence.

"You know who I am?" Maggot demanded.

Hickok slowly looked up at the pumpkin head glaring down at him. "From here, you look like a giant mound of horse shit. Paler, of course."

Everyone in the room glanced at Maggot, their faces terrified.

Maggot took the insult in stride. "You're a real smart ass, aren't you?"

"Proper grammar for once," Hickok cracked. "Hardly expected to find you were the literate type."

"My parents taught me to read and write," Maggot said, smiling, "just before I strangled them to death."

Hickok grinned at Maggot's feeble attempts at intimidation. "Too bad it wasn't the other way around." He picked up a spoon and tasted the watery soup. Yuck.

"A real smart ass," Maggot repeated. "I hear your name is Hickok."

Hickok glanced at Rat, who was grinning from ear to ear. "You got it correctly."

"Where you from?"

"I'd rather not say."

"Oh?" Maggot's fingers tightened on the Henry. "What if I insist?"

"You know what they say," Hickok said, trying another swallow of soup. It was better than nothing.

"No. What do they say?" Maggot asked, enjoying their game of cat and mouse.

"Insisting is a lot like playing with yourself."

"How so?"

Hickok grinned. "Neither do you any good unless you're sure you can get satisfaction out of them."

Maggot chuckled, his rolls of fat bouncing. "You've got a keen sense of humor, Hickok."

"Thanks."

"But a deplorable grasp on reality."

"Oh?" Hickok gulped the soup directly from the bowl. It was amazing how docile starvation could render your taste buds!

"Yes." Maggot began to pace. "You see, I'm accustomed to getting what I want, when I want it. I can make your life very pleasant, or I can make it very painful. The choice is yours, based on your degree of cooperation with me."

Hickok finished the soup, deliberately smacking his lips, pretending to ignore Maggot. "Not too bad. What was in it?"

"It was boiled rat," Rat answered.

Hickok felt his stomach jump and he nearly regurgitated his meal.

"Do you still refuse to tell me where you are from?" Maggot asked insistently.

"I sure do, pard. But . . ." Hickok lanquidly stretched. "I might answer your questions if you'll answer some of mine."

"I'm a reasonable man," Maggot announced. "What would you like to know?"

"About the Porns. Who are they? Where did they come from?"

"You're not from the Twins," Maggot stated, turning to the others. "Didn't I tell you?"

They all nodded.

"As far as your questions go," Maggot continued, "I can't answer all of them. There aren't many books left in the Twins. Most have been burned during the cold weather. From what my parents told me, and what I've learned on my own, the Porns began as a group of people who stayed behind in the Twins after the war. They took over the west part of the Twins for themselves, and they have been fighting the Horns ever since. That's the way things were until about seven years ago, when that damned Zahner started the Nomads. They took part of the Horns' turf away from them, set up their own territory, and vastly complicated our life.''

Hickok was puzzled, still lacking the answers he needed to understand the situation in the Twins. "Why are the Porns and Horns always fighting each other?"

"It's always been that way."

"But why? You need to have a reason to fight."

"You do?" Maggot grinned. "We don't. We love to kill the Horns! Those bastards look down their noses at us, like we're the scum of the earth! Them and their lousy God."

"Their God?"

Maggot raised the barrel of the Henry and smacked it into his right palm. "Enough from me," he said impatiently. "Now's time for you to come up with some answers."

Hickok nonchalantly placed his hand behind him and leaned back. "Okay. Shoot." He wondered how Maggot would react to what was coming.

"Where are you from?" Maggot asked.

"Somewhere else," Hickok casually replied.

"I know that! Where?"

"Deadwood."

"Deadwood?" Maggot repeated, frowning. "I never heard of it," he added doubtfully.

"You've never heard of Deadwood?" Hickok asked in fake astonishment.

"No. Where is it?"

Hickok tried to estimate the extent of Maggot's familiarity with geography and history. If the books were destroyed, Maggot's knowledge would be extremely limited. Maggot would have no way of knowing Wild Bill Hickok was shot and killed in Deadwood.

"Deadwood is west of here a ways," he answered.

"Really?" Maggot was naively buying the scam. "Who runs this Deadwood?"

"Two men." Hickok suppressed a grin. "The Lone Ranger and his faithful companion, Tonto."

"And why are you here?"

"We send people out from time to time," Hickok explained. "Scouting, hunting, and the like."

"Are you guys Watchers?" Maggot probed.

"Nope."

"Do you know where the Watchers are from?" Maggot interrogated.

"Sure don't," Hickok replied. "They're as much a mystery to us as they are to you."

Maggot paused, mulling the information.

"Anything else you want to know?" Hickok asked helpfully.

"Did you come here alone?"

"Naw. My good pard came with me."

"Who's that?"

"You don't know him. His name is Zane Grey."

Maggot's lower lip twitched. "Zane Grey? You don't say."

"You've heard of him?"

"As a matter of fact," Maggot stated slowly, "I have."

Hickok grinned. The fool! He was pretending to be knowledgeable to impress the others.

"I certainly have," Maggot hissed. Without warning, he bent and rammed the barrel of the Henry into Hickok's stomach.

Hickok doubled over, gasping for air, the soup gushing from his mouth and over the front of his buckskin shirt.

Maggot grabbed Hickok by the collar and jerked him to his feet. "You had me going, Hickok. I was falling for your shit until you mentioned Zane Grey.

You see, I told you that most of the books in the Twins have been used as fuel for our fires, but not all of them. I personally own a dozen. One of them is called *The Day of the Beast*, by a man named Zane Grey. Nice try, you son of a bitch!" He threw Hickok to the floor. "Take him to the pit!" he ordered. "We'll fix his ass! Permanently!"

15

He stood framed in the tent opening, the sun revealing his brown hair and blue eyes, his white skin tanned brown, wearing black shorts and leather sandals, and carrying one of their three rifles. In this case, a Marlin 336C, a six-shot lever action. He could drop a deer at two hundred yards with one shot.

"Hello, Bertha," he greeted her. He paused to tie the tent flap up, then entered.

Bertha tried to rise, but couldn't. She was lying on a worn mattress and was covered with blankets. Her right side was bandaged.

"Don't try to get up," he told her. "You've lost too much blood."

Bertha reached up and took his right hand in hers. "Z, it's good to see you again!" She smiled, her affection genuine. "I missed you."

Zahner sat down on the ground next to the mattress. "That's nice to hear. I missed you too. Listen, do you feel up to talking right now? I told them to get me as soon as you woke up."

"I can talk," she said. "I'm hungry, though. Sure would like some food."

"It's on its way," he assured her. Zahner pointed at her right side. "Sorry about that. The boys just didn't know if they could trust you or not."

Bertha frowned, glancing at the bandage. "I sure am gettin' the shit thumped out of me lately."

"Really? Mind telling me about it?"

"How long have I been out?" she asked.

"About two days."

"No!" She attempted to rise again, getting no further than her elbows before collapsing. "Damn!"

"What's the rush to get back on your feet?" Zahner closely watched her features, searching for the slightest hint of deception and treachery.

"I need to get back," she said, fuming over her debilitated condition. "He needs me."

"Who needs you?"

"Hickok. A friend of mine," she said guardedly.

Zahner stared into her eyes. "I thought we were your friends, Bertha."

"You are," she declared. "You're one of the best friends I've got."

"Then you've got to understand my position," Zahner said. "A lot of people count on me to make the right decisions, and I can't let them down. You know how it is, how it's been. I got so sick and tired of all the fighting between the Horns and the Porns I couldn't stand it anymore. You know I once was a Horn. You wouldn't believe how regimented they've become, how they try to control every aspect of your life. So I thought I'd break away and form my own group. That's how the Nomads were started. What amazed me was how many others wanted to join me once the word got out. Dozens and dozens from both sides. Any day now I half expect a Wack to waltz in and ask to join us."

Bertha grinned. She knew all this, so what was he driving at? It was difficult to concentrate on Zahner. Her mind was filled with fear for Hickok's safety and dread that he was dead.

"All these people relying on my judgment," Zahner was saying, his voice low, troubled. "I can't let them down. I thought forming my own group would solve all my problems, but it hasn't. The fighting hasn't stopped. It's become worse. Now the Porns and the Horns raid us, and we raid them. We're caught in the same stupid, vicious cycle they are."

Bertha, still worrying about Hickok, became aware Zahner had stopped. He was gazing at the ground, his eyes blank, dejected. "Hey, bro! Are you okay?" she asked him.

Zahner shook himself and smiled. "It gets to me sometimes, Bertha. You know what I mean?"

"I know where you're comin' from."

"So, anyway," he resumed, clearing his throat, "I came to the conclusion the only way we could escape this mess was to get out of the Twins. I picked my most trusted, capable soldier and I sent her out, hoping she could find a way out of the Twins."

Bertha recalled her determined reluctance to return to the Twins and she avoided his gaze, feeling humiliated and a disgrace to those who had counted on her.

Zahner noted her look. "It's been weeks, Bertha. Where the hell have you been? I was positive you'd been killed because of my harebrained scheme. Do you have any idea how bad I've felt? How many times I reproached myself for being a jerk?" His voice rose in anger. "Do you have any idea what you've put me through?"

"I'm really sorry," she apologized. "I didn't mean. . ." She stopped, faltering, overwhelmed by her betrayal. "I didn't think of it that way." She lowered her head, resisting an impulse to cry. Not her! No way!

Zahner came closer, sitting on the mattress next to her. "Hey, I'm sorry. I didn't want to upset you."

"It's okay," she sniffed. "I understand."

"I'll leave you alone and come back later." He started to rise.

Bertha grabbed his arm. "Don't, Z! Don't leave! I need to talk with someone."

"I've always been here whenever you needed me."

"I know. That's what makes it worse."

"How do you mean?"

She raised her head, her eyes rimmed with tears. "I wanted out of here so bad, I was ready and willin' to turn tail and desert you and the rest."

"It's all right," he tried to assure her.

"I was ready to wimp out on my friends," she went on as if she hadn't heard. "Now look at me!" she snapped bitterly.

"I really think you need to be alone."

"No. Look at me! I've lost my friends . . ."

"You haven't lost us. We might have doubted you, but you're still our friend."

" . . . and I've lost my ticket to freedom . . ."

"What do you mean?"

" . . . and the man I was comin' to love." She choked on the last words, reaching for him with her good arm.

Zahner, shocked, hugged her gently, stroking her hair. "It's okay, Bertha. Really. There's no need to get so upset. We forgive you."

"I don't know as I can forgive myself," she mumbled.

Zahner drew back, smiling, trying to cheer her. "You really need someone to talk to?"

"Damn straight."

"Then I'm all ears."

"Where do you want me to start?"

"At the beginning."

So she told him, every step of her journey, every gory detail, about her capture and subsequent sexual abuse and beatings, about the Family and the men she'd encountered, and about one man in particular, one man who had won her heart.

Zahner listened patiently, analyzing each detail, marveling. The telling took several hours. After hearing about the Family and the Home, the seed of an idea sprouted in Zahner's mind.

Bertha finally finished, weary, reclining on the mattress. "And that's it," she concluded. "The whole trip. You can still sit there and tell me you like me after what I did? What I was going to do?"

"Could a soul be blamed for wanting to escape the torment of hell? Don't be so hard on yourself. We've got more important matters to consider." His eyes, for the first time in weeks, lit with a spark of hope.

"I don't follow you."

"Oh, you will." He laughed. "You'll follow me all the way to our new home."

"New home?" she asked, stumped.

"Our new home." Zahner beamed. "The Home!"

16

He didn't know how long he'd been groping in the darkness, feeling his way foot by cautious foot, using his matches sparingly, only when absolutely necessary.

Great Spirit, was he to wander in this stinking maze until he dropped?

Geronimo stopped, his weariness nagging at his mind, needing to rest his head, close his eyes, and sleep.

The sounds returned, an ominous admonition that if he slept, he'd die.

Geronimo wanted to rub his tired eyes, but if he did, he'd smear the muck all over his face and burn his eyes. How long had it been since the Wack had lured him into the tunnels? He remembered falling, landing hard, twisting his right ankle, spraining the muscles. His flailing arms had touched his Browning, and he had grabbed it and risen to his feet. The girl had laughed at him. She had vanished, and he had heard scraping, and something had been pushed over the opening, sealing him in and plunging him into deepest blackness. He had tried to find a means of climbing out, but couldn't. Frustrated, he had begun to follow the tunnel he was in.

The experience was a living nightmare!

The tunnel's height varied, allowing him to walk erect for long stretches, and at other times forcing him to crawl through a reeking, clinging slime for interminable periods. The atmosphere was oppressive, dank and dismal. His knees and elbows were scraped raw, his sore ankle throbbed incessantly, and his stomach constantly reminded him of his gnawing hunger.

Then there were the sounds.

At first, there hadn't been any, only unnerving silence. He couldn't say exactly when he first became aware of the scratching and the squeaking. One moment he was crawling along a cramped passage, trying to suppress a growing claustrophobic fear, the only noise his labored breathing, and the next moment something behind him squealed in a high-pitched tone. He stopped and tried to peer over his shoulder, fruitlessly searching for the source. His eyes had adjusted to the darkness sufficiently to enable him to distinguish his immediate surroundings.

Later, he dozed off for a few minutes, and was startled awake by the sensation of tiny teeth nibbling at his left hand. He'd jerked his hand back and grabbed the matches, a box taken from the supplies confiscated from the Watchers in Thief River Falls. He hastily lit a match, and in the light of the flame he first saw the fiery, feral eyes glaring at him from the blackness ahead, red pinpoints of malevolent intelligence.

The rats.

Now, hours and hours or even days later, he was finding it difficult to muster the effort to resist his fatigue. He speculated on why the rats hadn't attacked. Their number had grown since the first solitary rat had found him and announced his presence with that piercing squeak.

Geronimo paused, glancing up. He'd been crawling for some time, but above him the top of the tunnel sloped upward, a patch of gray between him and the roof. He stood, his muscles tired, hurting, especially his sprained ankle. A subdued rustling filled the tunnel.

Time to light another match.

When he'd first lit a match after the nibbling incident, one pair of red eyes were staring at him. The next time he lit up, there were twenty eyes. The last time, sixty.

How many now?

Geronimo struck a match against the edge of the box and raised the match over his head.

Great Spirit!

There were too many eyes to count, a veritable wall of red dots confronting him. Why hadn't they attacked? What were they waiting for? He could feel goose pimples break out all over his skin. Maybe they were biding their time, knowing he couldn't escape, keeping tabs on their mobile lunch. Or supper. Or whatever. He was just thankful they moved aside when he approached, closing in behind him after he passed.

Geronimo shuffled forward, dreading he would inadvertently step on one of the rodents and precipitate a mass attack. The thought of hundreds of razor-sharp teeth tearing at his flesh appalled him.

There had to be a way out of this maze!

What were the others doing now? Had Blade been eaten by the Wacks? Had Hickok and Bertha survived and reached the SEAL? Was Joshua dead because of his negligence? It would serve him right if the rats got him!

Geronimo squinted, perplexed. Was it his exhausted imagination playing tricks on him, or did it appear to lighten ahead?

Something bumped against his right foot.

An accident?

Another small body brushed against his left foot. He walked faster, ignoring his ankle.

The rats abruptly began squeaking and chattering.

What was happening?

He was certain now, his pace quickening, as he realized there was a glimmer of light in the distance. Could it be a way to freedom?

A rat hit his left leg at the knee, pointed teeth slashing through his pants and tearing his skin.

Geronimo swung the Browning, connecting, sending the rodent sailing against the tunnel wall to his left.

Another rat leaped onto his right leg, its claws grabbing the fabric and holding fast, biting deep.

Geronimo smashed it aside with his right fist.

Two more rats launched themselves, attaching their filthy, furry forms to his thighs, cutting and tearing.

Geronimo ran, making for the light, pounding at the rodents affixed to his thighs, sensing the rats were preparing for an all-out assault, apparently to prevent him from reaching the lit area ahead.

All the more reason to reach it!

Squealing, its muscles like coiled springs, a rat struck him in the middle of his back, catching hold.

The rat on his right thigh fell, its head smashed to a pulp by his repeated blows.

Another rat pounced on his left arm, scrambling,

missing its grip, and dropping.

Geronimo's moccasined feet were stomping on rat after rat, kicking bodies in all directions.

Something brushed his right cheek.

The light was getting closer. Maybe forty yards to go.

More rats were connecting, coming at him from all sides.

He had to discourage them long enough to reach the light!

The rat on his back was chewing his flesh.

Geronimo fired the Browning as he ran, three blasts in front, scattering the rodents. He crouched and spun, shooting twice to his rear.

He was momentarily clear.

It was now or never!

Geronimo pounded along the tunnel, managing ten yards without another rat jumping him, then twenty, and thirty, and he could distinguish the tunnel widening at the end, joining a large room or chamber. The light was coming from that chamber.

A huge rat bounced off his chest.

Another gouged his left buttock.

Almost there!

Geronimo's feet contacted a scurrying rodent, and he tripped and sprawled the final five feet, falling forward, trying to catch hold of anything, failing, plunging headfirst into a pool of murky, pungent water, losing the Browning, and accidentally swallowing several mouthfuls of warm, acrid liquid. The taste was nauseating.

Sputtering and coughing, he broke the surface, shaking his head to clear his vision, expecting the rats to swarm all over him.

They were gone.

Geronimo's legs brushed bottom, and he

discovered he could stand, the water level at his waist.

The rats were gone!

He stared at the tunnel he'd emerged from, amazed. Where had they gone? Why had they stopped when they almost had him?

A sharp, searing pain in his lower back reminded him that one rat, at least, was still with him. He reached behind his back with his left hand, his fingers closing on a slippery, hairy form. The rodent screeched as he squeezed and tore it from his back, bringing it around in front of him.

The rat twisted and squirmed, struggling to get loose, glaring at Geronimo, the long front teeth rising and falling as the mouth opened and closed.

Contemptuously, he tossed the rat into the water.

The rodent rose to the surface and began swimming away from him, its legs jerking as it swam.

Geronimo surveyed his deliverance. It was a spacious chamber, seventy-five yards across, filled with water. Several access tunnels emptied into it. The roof was thirty feet above his head. Litter and rubble clogged the surface of the pond, the trash so thick in many spots he couldn't see the water. The light streamed in from an opening in the roof at the far end of the chamber. Metal rungs imbedded in the wall rose from the pond to the opening.

Sunlight! Precious sunlight! It had never looked so good!

Geronimo smiled, relieved. The ordeal was over! He'd find some food and return to where he'd left Joshua.

The rat was halfway across the pond, bearing for the far side and another access tunnel.

Good riddance!

Geronimo scoured the brackish water for the

Browning. He bent over and groped below the surface, averse to diving in the polluted water, recognizing he wouldn't be able to see more than an inch or two anyway. He tried running his feet along the spongy bottom to no avail.

The Browning was gone.

He sighed, disappointed. True, the Family owned a literal armory, but the loss of any firearm was tragic because it could never be replaced. The munitions factories had long since been idled. Or had they? After all, the Watchers owned new guns.

A commotion erupted behind him, loud splashing and a squeak.

Geronimo turned, noting concentric ripples covering the surface thirty yards away. There was no sign of the rat. The lure of the beckoning sunlight goaded him to head for the opening. The sooner he was out of here, the better!

Garbage blocked his path at several points. He swept it away with his forearm, moving slowly, his feet tentatively taking one measured step after another. He was leery of dropping into a sinkhole, unwilling to submerge again.

Geronimo frowned, realizing their trip to the Twin Cities had turned into one giant fiasco. Plato might have had the right idea, but the execution left considerable to be desired. What chance was there that any of the equipment Plato required was in the Twins, let alone functional? The probability was very slim. The Twin Cities were a monumental ruin and an actual madhouse. It was no wonder Bertha had wanted to stay away, to not come back. Who could blame her? She'd been right, after all. Why was it, he reflected, a person could only learn things the hard way? Was it simply human nature?

A motion to his right caught his attention.

Geronimo stopped and watched, bewildered, as a

clump of debris moved rapidly across the pond for ten yards before coming to a stop.

What in the world? Was there something else in this water?

The thought spurred him on. He walked faster, the water level rising a bit, reaching his chest.

A frog croaked to his left.

A frog! Geronimo relaxed, feeling ridiculous. Why wouldn't there be amphibians and even fish in this pond? It was polluted, but not too severely.

Another cluster of litter blocked his path, surrounding a long, pitted piece of wood. He reached for the wood and shoved, amazed when it continued to move of its own volition.

The creature erupted in a frenzy, whipping a long tail in an arc and slamming Geronimo in the head, churning the water as it twisted and lunged at him.

Geronimo fell sideways, stunned, glimpsing a protruding tapered snout, two yellowish-green, bulging eyes, and a gaping maw filled with a seemingly endless number of teeth.

Teeth!

17

"So tell me, smart ass," Maggot mocked him. "Have you got anything to say now?"

Hickok's body slowly turned, first one direction, then another, as the rope securing him to the beam twisted. Rat was lying on the beam, spinning the rope, deriving satisfaction from trying to make Hickok dizzy.

"The accommodations leave a little to be desired, fatso," Hickok taunted his captor.

Maggot, standing on the rim of the pit with his four bodyguards and Bear, frowned. "We'll see if you're so flippant after the rats come for their meal. You'll be a long time dying."

"Not as long as you would take, blubber breath." Hickok grinned. "The rats could feast on your carcass for a year or more!"

Maggot started to raise the Henry, then thought better of it. "No," he said. "I want you to go slow. I want you to feel them eating your flesh from the feet up. I want to come back here later and see the fear in your eyes!"

Hickok deliberately yawned.

"Very funny," Maggot snapped.

"I have a question," Hickok stated.

"Oh?"

"Yeah," Hickok said, his wrists beginning to ache from the strain of supporting his entire weight. "If you kill me, how the blazes do you think you'll get the answers you want?"

"Do I look stupid?" Maggot angrily demanded.

"Does a bear shit in the woods?"

"Keep it up," Maggot said. "When I get back, you'll beg me to cut you loose. You'll tell me everything I want to know, and I won't need to lift a finger."

"Just so it's not your arm."

Maggot, about to leave, was taken off stride by the remark. "What do you mean by that?"

"Ever heard of something called personal hygiene?"

Hickok noticed that Bear looked away from Maggot and grinned.

Maggot didn't find the joke funny. "So long, you lousy son of a bitch!" He strode off.

"Your mother!" was all Hickok could think of. Brilliant repartee, he told himself.

The bodyguards and Bear followed Maggot.

"Come on!" Maggot ordered Rat.

"Just a minute." Rat carefully stood on the beam. The wood was six inches across and he maintained his balance easily. He reached for some buttons at his crotch.

What in the world? Hickok asked himself.

He got his answer.

Perched on the beam, laughing inanely, Rat emptied his urinary bladder on Hickok.

As the first drops struck his hair and shoulders, Hickok lowered his face and held his breath. The bastard! The crummy bastard! He'd get him, if it was the last thing he ever did!

The downpour ceased.

"Hey, Hickok?" Rat called down to him. "Ever hear of personal hygiene?"

Hickok could hear the others laughing as Rat joined them. This was followed by the loud slamming of a door.

Well, he mentally congratulated himself, this was yet another superb mess he'd fallen into! So what was next?

Hickok studied his predicament.

Maggot had suspended him in a circular, earthen pit twelve feet in diameter and ten feet deep. At the bottom of the pit, illuminated by two torches imbedded in the ground at the top of the pit, were three black holes. Tunnels. To where? It really didn't matter. The important point was that rats would be coming out of those tunnels to devour him, a particularly unsavory prospect if ever there was one! The pit was located in a barren room in the basement of the building the Porns used as their headquarters. He hadn't seen much of it when they hauled him down flights of stairs to his room, still reeling from Maggot's blow to his gut. They'd passed other Porns, who scurried out of the way and fearfully minded their own business. Maggot's rule was predicated on intimidation, a fact Hickok intended to use to his advantage when he escaped from the pit.

When?

Who was he kidding?

If.

Hickok wondered where, exactly, he was being held. How far was it from the SEAL? What had happened to Bertha and the others? Were any of them still alive?

A high-pitched squeak came from below.

Hickok glanced down.

A rat was directly below him, staring up, its whiskers and nose twitching.

"Beat it, hair ball!" Hickok shouted.

The rat scurried into one of the tunnels.

Hickok smiled. Score one for the idiot! Thank the Spirit, he still had his guns! They'd dragged him to the pit, holding him under his armpits, his feet bumping down each and every step as they descended to the basement. Brother, did they smart! Fortunately, the Porns had missed his concealed guns. When they bound his wrists, one of the bodyguards had held him fast at the elbows and another had tied the rope at the edge of his wrists, at the point where they joined the hands. They'd walked him onto the beam and wrapped the other end of the rope around the wood, knotting it securely. Then, Maggot chuckling, they had shoved him from the beam. His shoulders had lanced with agony when he reached the end of the rope, causing him to grit his teeth to suppress a scream. He hadn't been about to give them the satisfaction! Instead, he had smiled up at Maggot, and detected a dawning reflection of fear in Maggot's eyes.

More squeals came from underneath his dangling feet.

Hickok looked down again.

Now there were two rats.

"Brought your wife, did you?" Hickok said to the rodents. "Why don't you go home and get the kids? Make a family night out of it, for crying out loud."

Two more rats emerged from one of the black holes.

Uh-oh!

Time for Mama Hickok's little darling to get the hell out of here!

Hickok watched the gathering rodents. Now there

were seven. His feet were about two feet above the floor of the pit, within their reach if they jumped high enough. He glanced up at the beam. There were two feet of rope between his hands and the bottom of the beam. Not much to work with, but it would have to do.

One of the rats, hungrier than the rest, leaped, smacking against his right foot and dropping to the ground.

"You can do better than that, gruesome," he told the rodent.

The same rat tried again, missing.

Determined little fart!

Hickok concentrated, his muscles throbbing, and gripped the rope with his hands. Good. Step one completed.

A rat struck his left foot, clinging for an instant, then falling.

Hickok began moving his legs back and forth in an increasingly wider pendulum motion, his momentum building. He kept at it until his long legs were almost parallel with the beam. Perfect! Tightening his stomach muscles, he swept his legs as high as he could force them, wrapping his calves around the beam and in one fluid motion swinging up and onto the beam, desperately clamping his elbows and thighs against the wood, fearful for an instant he would lose his hold.

He didn't!

Hickok smiled at his success. Step two completed. He was out of the pit and precariously poised on the wooden beam. So now what? He was still tied to the beam, bound at the wrists. How did he expect to get loose? He gazed down at the gathering rats, an idea occurring. Maybe he could chew through the rope and free his hands. He examined the rope, dismayed. It was at least a half-inch thick and constructed from a sturdy synthetic. Fat chance he could bite through it. Besides, he reflected, there was another reason he wasn't about to touch his mouth to the rope. Rat's . . . watering . . . had covered his hands and the knot. He wasn't about to let his lips come in contact with something Rat had pissed on.

So what to do?

First things first. If Maggot or one of the other Porns suddenly returned, he would be powerless to resist, too exposed on the beam. He needed an edge, but could he do it and still keep his balance? Only one way to find out.

Piece of cake, he told himself.

Slowly, exercising supreme care, Hickok drew his legs up closer to his body until his knees were touching his elbows. His legs now had a firm clasp on the beam, and he laboriously rose to a sitting position. Hallelujah! He reached his hands down, raised the buckskin covering his left leg to just above his ankle, and unsnapped the catch on the small holster for the C.O.P. .357 Magnum. Grinning, he drew the gun and sat up again.

Now let the bastards come!

As if on cue, the door abruptly opened.

Hickok swiveled, leveling the C.O.P., his finger tightening on the trigger.

Bear, just inside the doorway, threw his hands in the air, holding the Winchester in his left fist.

"Hey!" Bear said hastily. "Don't shoot, Hickok! I'm here to help you!"

"Close the door!" Hickok commanded harshly.

Bear complied.

"Lay that Winchester on the ground."

"You got it!" Bear began to bend over.

"Slowly!"

Bear made a show of placing the rifle on the ground, his movements measured, conveying his lack of hostile intent.

"Now stand up and come over here," Hickok directed, his gun steady in his grip.

Bear walked over to the edge of the pit, smiling.

"What's so funny?" Hickok wanted to know.

"You, bro. You." Bear laughed.

"How do you mean?"

"You sure are somethin'," Bear stated in admiration. "Maggot made a big mistake when he didn't kill you right off."

"Thanks."

"I'm tryin' to tell you," Bear said sincerely, looking Hickok in the eyes, "that I think you got a lot of guts. You're one mean dude, Hickok."

Hickok smiled. "I already know that."

"Yes, sir." Bear nodded his head. "Maybe Maggot's finally met his match."

"What are you doing here?" Hickok asked.

"I came to set you free," Bear explained.

"Like you did Bertha?" Hickok casually remarked.

Bear's mouth fell. "How'd you know that?"

"It wasn't too hard to figure out," Hickok replied. "The question is, why are you helping me?"

"Ain't it plain?" Bear frowned. "I hate Maggot!" he snapped, venom in his words.

"I take it you're not the only one?"

"Hell, no!" Bear gestured toward the building above them. "Nearly everybody hates him! He's the meanest leader the Porns ever had! He's pure scum!"

"If everyone hates him so much," Hickok said, broaching a subject he'd mentioned before, "why doesn't someone simply blow him away?"

"Don't think some haven't tried!" Bear glanced at the door. "It just ain't that easy, is all. Like I told you before, Maggot never lets anyone get close to him with a weapon, 'less they is one of his inner circle, and only they get to pack the rods."

"You're one of his trusted lieutenants," Hickok observed.

"I'm the token."

"The what?"

"The token, man."

Hickok went to ask a question, then thought of a higher priority. "You got a knife?"

"Right here." Bear patted his left rear pocket.

"Cut me free," Hickok ordered.

Bear hurriedly complied, clambering onto the beam to remove the rope from Hickok's wrists.

When he was once again on terra firma, Hickok rubbed his aching wrists, thankful to be out of the pit. "Thanks," he said simply.

"Don't think nothin' of it," Bear responded. "You'd do the same for me."

"You think so?"

"I know so."

Hickok grinned. "Do you expect the others back here soon?"

Bear shook his head. "Not for a while. Maggot's eatin', and he don't let nothin' disturb him when he's feedin' that fat face of his."

"Good. So we got some time on our hands. Tell me, what's a token?"

"You puttin' me on?" Bear eyed him quizzically.

"What's a token?" Hickok repeated.

"I'll try and explain," Bear answered. "You see, there's a lot of black Porns, almost as many as there are whites. Maggot ain't too fond of black skin, but he don't let it show or he'd have a revolt on his hands. So to keep all the other blacks happy, and make them believe he's all right, he made me one of his bodyguards. I didn't know the truth myself until after I got to know him."

"He doesn't like blacks." Hickok considered this new information, pondering how he could use it to his advantage. "But you said Maggot wanted to . . . sleep . . . with Bertha."

"Maggot will screw anything," Bear informed him. "Anything."

"How'd Maggot get to be top dog here?"

"He did the same as all the other heads have done," Bear replied.

"What's that?"

"He killed the one who was the leader before him."

"Oh? Democratic group, aren't you?"

"What?"

"Nothing. What happens if Maggot is killed?"

Bear's face lit up. "How do you mean?"

"Who assumes command if Maggot is killed?"

"Whoever kills him," Bear answered.

"What if an outsider did it?"

"You don't understand the Porns," Bear said wearily. "Most of us are tired of bein' bossed around, told what to do and when to do it. We're tired of fightin' the Horns and the Nomads, and scrapin' to just stay alive."

"Why don't they change the way things are?"

"They're just too scared," Bear said, eyeing Hickok hopefully, "and they haven't got someone to show them any different."

Hickok walked to the Winchester and picked it up.

"You got a plan?" Bear asked.

"Yep."

"Mind fillin' me in on it?"

Hickok stared at the door. There wouldn't be any other cover when they came. The basement room was empty, devoid of furniture, and lacked a floor. He had the impression the room had been under construction at the time of the Big Blast. Why else would they have left a room with a dirt foundation?

"Bear." Hickok faced him. "When Maggot comes, how many you figure he'll bring with him?"

"No telling," Bear admitted. "At least his four bodyguards. He's got more guards, but the four you saw are his special ones. Maggot don't go nowhere without them. A couple more might tag along, like Rat."

"I hope Rat comes," Hickok stated in a quiet, hard tone.

"But if he decides to show you off," Bear added, "he might bring a whole bunch with him."

"That would be too bad." Hickok approached the door, noting it swung inward to admit entry. Good. "Can I rely on you?" he glanced at Bear.

"Me?"

"You going to help me fight?"

"I don't know . . ." Bear said hesitantly.

"You said you hated Maggot," Hickok reminded him.

"I do."

"And remember what he did to Bertha."

"I ain't forgettin'," Bear said.

"So what's wrong?" Hickok demanded. "You don't strike me as the yellow type."

"I ain't a wimp, if that's what you mean," Bear said testily.

"So I can count on you?"

"I don't know, Hickok. I ain't too fond of committing suicide."

"Suicide?"

Bear fidgeted, nervously toying with his pants, pulling at the fabric and running his hands up and down.

"Can I count on you or not?" Hickok pressed him.

"You just don't know what he's like," Bear

replied. "If we miss, he'll torture us for sure. You should have seen some of the things he's done! Once, a guy tried to waste Maggot and was caught tryin'. Maggot hacked off the guy's balls and force-fed them to the poor son of a bitch! The way that man screamed! It was terrible!" Bear shuddered with the recollection.

"It's okay," Hickok told him. "If you don't want to help, you don't have to."

"I mean," Bear said, to himself more than Hickok, "helpin' you get away is one thing. Goin' up against Maggot is another."

"I understand," Hickok assured him.

"You say you got a plan?" Bear asked optimistically.

"Sure do."

"What the hell is it?"

Hickok grinned. "I'm going to wait here until Maggot and his cronies return, and then I'm going to kill them."

"Just like that, huh?"

"Just like that."

Bear chuckled. "And what if they kill you?"

"Then bury me on boot hill, pard."

"What?"

"Never mind." Hickok tossed the Winchester to Bear. "Stay or go. It's your decision."

"You're crazy, sucker! You know that?"

Hickok nodded. "I've been told that once or twice."

Bear took a deep breath. "So what do you want me to do?"

18

He was reclining on a comfortably made bed in a spacious room illuminated by sunlight streaming in through four windows, one in the center of each wall. Colorful blue draperies hung on the windows. A worn blue rug covered the wooden floor. Beside the bed stood an oak table, the leftovers from his last meal on top.

Joshua sighed, at ease. His head had been meticulously tended to and bandaged, and they had changed his clothes, providing some of the typical garments they wore, a black shirt and pants.

The door opened and in walked a short, bearded man with gray hair, narrow features, and a pronounced limp.

"How are you feeling, Brother Joshua?" asked the newcomer.

"Just fine," Joshua confided. "I can't thank you enough, Reverend Paul, for all you have done for me."

"Please, just call me Paul." The Reverend, likewise attired in black, sat on the foot of the bed.

"I can't thank you enough," Joshua reiterated. "I

never expected to find such kindness in the Twin Cities after my initial experiences."

"Don't thank us." Paul held up a gold necklace, consisting of Joshua's cross and chain. "Thank this. If my alert brethren hadn't found this when they were searching you, they would have left you there for the animals to devour."

"A cross made that much difference?"

"A cross makes all the difference!" Paul stated emphatically. "Our Master went to his reward from a cross." He stared at the Latin cross on the chain. "The heathen would never wear a symbol like this! They have entered sinful ways! They are evil."

"By the heathen," Joshua said, "I take it you mean the Porns you told me a bit about?"

"Of course!" Paul's vibrant voice rose. "Who else? But then," he quickly added apologetically, "I must remember you are not from the Twins. Astonishing!"

"No, I'm not from the Twins," Joshua said softly, "and I'd like to know more about them. I've answered all your questions concerning how I came here and where I came from . . . ."

"Incredible!" Paul interrupted. "Praise the Lord! He has sent you to us, Brother Joshua. We would never have expected that there is another group who believes as we do."

"We believe in the Supreme," Joshua said, selecting his words with the utmost discretion, "and we are taught that all men and women are brothers and sisters."

"Praise the Lord!" Paul exclaimed happily.

"And I've already told you about the Family and the Home," Joshua continued. "Now, I would be pleased if you would consent to answering some questions I have about the Twin Cities."

"I would be glad to do so," Paul said heartily.

"Can you tell me how the current situation came about?" Joshua inquired. "Do you have any idea of the history of the Twin Cities since the war?"

"I know it all," Paul said proudly.

"You do?"

"Of course." Paul gazed at the white ceiling, sorting his facts. "Each leader of the First Church has kept a journal of events, beginning with Reverend Jack Wilcox, our illustrious organizer, the man who established the First Church of the Nazarene."

They had touched briefly on this subject the night before. "He was the one who refused to evacuate when the Government gave the order to leave the Twin Cities?" Joshua asked.

"Exactly. Reverend Wilcox was a true fundamentalist, and he was a great man, with profound faith in the Word. He knew his flock had nothing to worry about, and he called on them to stay here with him, to show the sinful world that there were Christians willing to commit themselves, totally, to their Lord, and to rely on Him to preserve them in times of crisis. Bless them! Most of them saw the light and stayed! Two hundred and ninety-four souls stood firm and stayed in the church, praying to their Maker, while panic filled the streets and the populace fled. And here we have stayed, ever since, never leaving St. Paul. We have withstood the onslaughts of the degenerates and the wicked! We have stayed true to the Word!"

"How many of you are there now?" Joshua asked Paul.

"Let's see." Paul calculated a moment. "I would say upwards of four hundred."

"You have prospered over the years, I take it?"

"Of course! The Lord looks after His own."

"How many of the other groups are there? The

Porns and the Nomads and the Wacks?"

"I can't answer with complete certainty," Paul said. "But I would estimate there are close to six hundred Porns, damn their souls! They're filthy creatures, little better than an animal in their moral and spirutal status."

Joshua noted that comment for subsequent deliberation. "What about the Nomads and the Wacks?"

"The Nomads were only formed seven years ago," Paul stated sadly, his face downcast, "by one of our own brethren. Zahner is his name. He and I were close. I can't understand why he did what he did."

"How many follow Zahner?"

"Surprisingly, our estimates place the Nomad population at two hundred or so."

"Why does that surprise you?"

Paul frowned. "It reveals that many apparently feel the way Zahner does."

"How does he feel?"

Paul leaned on his right elbow. "He left the First Church because he said he was tired of the constant warfare between us and the Porns."

"Which prompts another question," Joshua said continuing his probe. "Why do you call them the Porns? And why do they call you the Horns? And what about the Wacks?"

"Let's see." Paul idly picked at the blanket Joshua was lying on. "Taking them one at a time, in sequence," he said, revealing his information, "starting with the vile Porns, our journals tell us that Reverend Wilcox was not the only one who remained in the Twin Cities. Another man, a dealer in pornography and other diverse wickedness, a man with an organized criminal empire, an owner of what were known as porno movie houses and massage parlors and a previously convicted dealer in drugs, also stayed. This man was named Creel. His

businesses were established along Lake Street and
Hennepin Avenue in Minneapolis, and he refused to
leave. Many of his criminal cohorts stuck with him,
his muscle men and the pimps and the whores and
the addicts and the rest. There they are to this day,
breeding like rabbits!"

"Fascinating," Joshua said, amazed. "So
Minneapolis was taken over by this pornographer,
Creel, and St. Paul by the First Church, two groups
with diametrically opposed views and lifestyles."

"Precisely," Paul confirmed. "At first, the two
sides managed to live in peaceful coexistence, until
the fateful day when one of the Porns raped one of
our young women. The Porns refused to turn the
culprit over for proper punishment, so the First
Church retaliated, attacking their camp and
destroying part of their food supply."

"And let me guess," Joshua finished. "The Porns
then took revenge on the First Church, and the First
Church had to have retribution, and reprisal
followed reprisal until the two sides came to hate
each other."

"There's more to it than that," Paul said stiffly.

"If I comprehend this," Joshua reasoned, "the
pornographers became known as the Porns. Am I
right?"

Paul nodded. "I don't know who first started it,
but at one point in his journal Reverend Wilcox
began referring to Creel and his ilk as Porns."

"But how did the First Church become known as
the Horns?"

"They did it."

"The Porns?"

"Yes. Again, my information in this respect is
sketchy, but evidently the Porns began referring to
us as self-righteous, vain, and intolerant. Imagine
that!"

"Yes, imagine that." Joshua suppressed a grin.

"Anyway, at one point they began casting aspersions on our physical sharing . . ."

"On your sex lilfe?"

Paul's face reddened. "Yes. They said our morality had repressed our human sexuality."

"They called you horny?" Joshua, at last, saw the light. The slang word was infrequently used by the male Family members, usually when the Warriors were gathered, reveling in their machismo humor. Telling jokes was a popular entertainment. Come to think of it, the last time he'd heard the word was when Hickok was telling a tale about a Warrior who'd encountered a beautiful woman in the woods and didn't know what to do with her because he'd failed the Family course in Sexual Organs: Their Function in Reproduction, a course taught by a senior Family couple. Joshua had overheard Hickok telling the story and, despite his initial embarrassment, he'd laughed his head off. Hickok was a gifted storyteller when he was in the mood. Where was Hickok at this very instant? And Blade, and Geronimo, and Bertha? Had the Wacks killed them? He realized Paul was speaking.

" . . . and we became known as the Horns to them. We never use the word ourselves, you understand?"

"Of course. Thank you for telling me this. It explains a lot. That leaves only the Wacks."

"Ahhh, yes. The poor lunatics."

"How do you mean?"

"From what the records reveal," Paul explained, "when the Government called for everyone to evacuate, everyone did, as quickly as they could. The entire staff at the Minnesota Hospital for the Criminally Insane, set up a few years before the war in Bloomington, in south Minneapolis, deserted their charges and left them to fend for themselves."

"Dear Father!"

"Indeed." Paul nodded. "The mentally depraved inmates took over the Hospital, and have flourished, scrounging like savage animals, ever since."

"But why are they called the Wacks?" Joshua still didn't comprehend their name.

"The Porns started it."

"How?"

Paul sighed. "The Porns have a remarkable facility for devising quaint terms for everything. Part of their street heritage, I believe. They began calling the insane ones the Wacks, a derivative of the word wacky, possibly, or of one of their obnoxious gutter expressions, wacko."

"At last." Joshua sat up, grimacing as the back of his head twinged with pain.

"At last what?"

"At last I have a glimmer of understanding as to how things reached the deplorable state they're in here in the Twin Cities." Joshua leaned back, resting against the headboard. "Now all that remains is to develop a viable solution."

"A solution to what?"

"A solution that will have everyone in the Twin Cities living as true sons and daughters of God should."

Paul's eyebrows arched. "You can't be serious?"

"I am."

Paul laughed. "Perhaps the blow to your head caused internal damage!"

"Why do you say that?"

"You can't really expect us to try and live in harmony with the Porns? Or even the Nomads, for that matter?"

"I do expect it." Joshua nodded slowly. "It is your duty to reach out to them in friendship and brotherhood."

Paul rose to his feet. "Says who?" he demanded, annoyed.

"Says our Master," Joshua stated solemnly.

"What?"

"Jesus left us with specific instructions regarding situations exactly like what you have here in the Twin Cities."

"What are you referring to?" Paul asked skeptically.

"Do you have any Bibles?"

"Of course," Paul stated. "We have quite a collection of sacred literature and other books. The stupid Porns burned most of the books in Minneapolis, and wherever else they found any. Once we became aware of what they were doing, we tried to salvage as many books as we could. We keep them under guard at the former Harding High School. I don't think the Porns even know we have them, or they would have tried a raid by now."

"But you have a Bible in this building?"

"Certainly. I'll go downstairs and get mine." Paul walked to the door.

"Say, Paul," Joshua said before Paul could exit. "I've been meaning to inquire about where I am in St. Paul?"

"Oh. You're in one of the buildings we maintain on the campus of Concordia College. There are far too many buildings in St. Paul for us to keep them all in useable condition, so we preserve certain ones, the ones best suited to our purposes. I'll get the Word." Paul departed.

Joshua folded his hands on his lap, trying to stay calm, to control his excitement. After reviewing his recent conduct, he considered his performance more of a detriment than an asset to Blade and the others. He viewed his contributions on the two runs in a negative light. What good had he done them? He'd protested every time the Warriors had defended them. He'd whined and moaned whenever they'd killed someone. Sure, he had saved Bertha from the Brute, but felt miserable afterwards. In the fight against the Wacks, he'd only been of minimal assistance. This might be his golden opportunity to achieve a positive goal, to reconcile the Horns and the Porns and end their incessant bloodshed. The Twin Cities were large enough for both groups, and the Nomads, to live side by side without trying to exterminate one another. If he could succeed in attaining a state of peace between the various factions, he'd feel as if he'd been of some small benefit on his journey. Was it possible, though? Was he being realistic or idealistic? After all, the Horns and the Porns had been contending for close to a century, and he recognized how difficult a task it was to alter human behavior once that conduct had become habitual. His one ray of hope was the statement about Zahner and the Nomads. If a couple of hundred had already joined Zahner, former Porns and Horns, it seemed to indicate that maybe, just maybe, the general populations on both sides really wanted peace. Maybe the Porns and the Horns wanted to terminate their conflict and get about the business of making the Twin Cities a better place in which to live.

Paul came into the room, waving a Bible in his right hand. "Here it is! Now you show me why I should extend friendship to the Porns!"

"Gladly." Joshua took the Bible. "But if I convince you, will you help me to persuade the other members of the First Church? Will they listen to us?"

Paul sat down on the edge of the bed. "They will listen to me! I am their leader and spiritual guide."

"All of us have a spiritual guide within us," Joshua said to Paul. "The Spirit is in each of us, trying to show us God's way, to reveal the Lord's path for us." He turned the pages, searching for the passage he wanted. "Tell me. How strongly do you believe in the words of Jesus?"

"With my heart and soul and mind and strength," Paul said indignantly. "I am a shepherd to His flock."

Joshua was still looking for the quote he needed. "So you believe that whatever Jesus said takes unqualified precedence over anything else in the Bible?"

"Jesus was the Word made flesh," Paul stated. "He is to be obeyed without question. Jesus is the fulfillment of prophecy."

"True," Joshua agreed.

"But what did you mean by what you said a second ago?" Paul inquired, intrigued by Joshua's audacity in lecturing *him* on Scripture, and impressed by Joshua's dignity, his concern, and his evident faith. "There are no contradictions in the Bible."

"Oh." Joshua stopped flipping the pages. "For instance, take Psalm One."

"Psalm One?"

"Verses Five and Six." Joshua ran his finger under the lines as he read. " 'Therefore the ungodly shall not stand in the judgment, nor sinners in the congregation of the righteous. For the Lord knoweth the way of the righteous; but the way of the ungodly shall perish,' " he quoted.

Paul smiled in satisfaction. "See! What did I tell you? That applies to the Porns if anything does!"

"Wait a moment." Joshua hurriedly turned to the

New Testament. "I'm not done yet. I know you are intimately familiar with the Scriptures, so I'll simply quote several passages and let you tell me if they also apply to the Porns. Fair enough?"

"Go ahead," Paul grinned. "But you won't change my mind."

"I'm not going to," Joshua replied. "Jesus is."

"Oh?"

Joshua quickly turned from one reference to another. "Let's start with Luke, Chapter Four, Verse Eighteen." He read the excerpt slowly. " 'The Spirit of the Lord is upon me, because he hath anointed me to preach the gospel to the poor; he hath sent me to heal the broken-hearted, to preach deliverance to the captives, and recovering of sight to the blind, to set at liberty them that are bruised.' " Joshua glanced at Paul. "Does this apply to you as well?"

"Of course. I am a minister to His fold. I must follow in his footsteps."

"Good." Joshua smiled. "Then let's keep going." He continued turning pages. "Remember when the scribes and the Pharisees became upset and asked why Jesus ate and drank with the sinners and the publicans?"

"Of course."

"From Luke, Chapter Five, Verses Thirty-one and Thirty-two," Joshua said. " 'They that are whole need not a physician; but they that are sick. I came not to call the righteous, but sinners to repentance.' " He scanned the next page. "And listen to Chapter Six, Verses Thirty-five, Thirty-six, and Thirty-seven." He shot a look at Paul, pleased at his furrowed brow and thoughtful countenance. " 'But love ye your enemies, and do good, and lend, hoping for nothing again; and your reward shall be great, and ye shall be the children of the Highest: for

173

he is kind unto the unthankful and to the evil. Be ye
therefore merciful, as your Father also is merciful.
Judge not, and ye shall not be judged: condemn not,
and ye shall not be condemned: forgive, and ye shall
be forgiven.' "

Paul reached up and scratched his chin. "I'm
aware of these teachings . . ." he began.

"But you refuse to apply them to the Porns?"
Joshua interrupted.

"Our situation is unique," Paul responded. "We
are . . ." He fell silent, gazing absently at the floor.

Joshua turned to John, Chapter Five, Verse
Twenty-four. " 'Verily, verily, I say unto you, He
that heareth my word, and believeth on him that
sent me, hath everlasting life, and shall not come
into condemnation, but is passed from death unto
life.' "

"They are our enemies," Paul said softly. "They
are."

Joshua found Chapter Ten, Verse Nine. " 'I am
the door: by me if any man enter in, he shall be
saved, and shall go in and out, and find pasture.'
Note that Jesus stresses 'any man.' "

"True," Paul said, struggling with an intense,
personal revelation.

Joshua tried another quote, from Chapter Twelve,
Verses Forty-six and Forty-seven, in John. " 'I am
come a light into the world, that whosoever
believeth on me should not abide in darkness. And if
any man hear my words, and believe not, I judge
him not: for I came not to judge the world, but to
save the world.' "

Paul stared at Joshua with fresh respect. "You
certainly know the Scriptures."

"I have spent the greater portion of my life studying the Bible and other special writings."

"I am impressed," Paul conceded.

Joshua leaned toward Paul. "Are you impressed enough to send an envoy to the Porns and request a meeting to iron out your differences?"

"They would laugh in our faces."

"You don't know that."

"They'll kill anyone we sent," Paul objected.

"But if someone did go, and they agreed to meet with you, would you talk to them?" Joshua said, pressing.

Paul nodded, very slowly. "Yes. I would. If there is any chance we can reach a peace, I am bound by my allegiance to our Lord to try it."

"Good."

"But you won't find anyone willing to go," Paul remonstrated. "No one wants to die uselessly. I'd go, Brother Joshua, but they would kill me on sight. Their current leader, Maggot, has boasted he will crucify me on a flaming cross."

"It was I who convinced you to attempt a reconciliation with the Porns." Joshua reached out and placed his right hand on Paul's left shoulder. "I wouldn't think of requesting that you impose on one of your brethren, or asking that you jeopardize your own safety."

"Then who will be the envoy you mentioned?"

"I will."

"What?" Paul stood, gesticulating with his arms. "You will not! I won't allow it."

"You have no other option."

"Yes I do. I can forbid you to go."

"I am not a member of the First Church," Joshua reminded Paul. "Rightfully, you lack authority over my actions."

Paul vigorously shook his head. "No. You don't understand. It is precisely because you are not of the First Church that I can't allow you to go. Don't you see?" Paul began nervously pacing the floor.

"All these years of trying to maintain our moral and spiritual integrity in the face of civilization's decay have exacted a horrid emotional toll on us. In recent years, I have detected a growing restlessness in my congregation. Their collective faith and enthusiasm is faltering, and who can fault them? We struggle for the basic necessities, hunting what little game there is, salvaging what we can from the ruins of the city, growing meager quantities of food where feasible, and resisting the depredations of the Porns and the Wacks and the animals. The one essential element conducive to spiritual growth we lack, and that is peace, the peace necessary to pursue our lives without hindrance and interference."

"What does all this have to do with your forbidding my going to the Porns with a peace proposal?" Joshua asked.

Paul ceased his pacing, his shoulders sagging. "My flock believes in the reality of our Lord and our eventual reward on high. This cherished hope sustains us in our travail. What we don't have, however, is a hope for our immediately earthly future. What do we have to look forward to? A lifetime of interminable conflict, periodic bouts with rampant disease, and, more often than not, a slow, painful death. But you change all this!"

"How?"

"You are our hope for our earthly future!" Paul exclaimed. "Just knowing that there is another group somewhere, similar to us in their beliefs, is immensely encouraging. It means we are not alone in this world! Can't you see how much that would mean to us?"

"I believe I can," Joshua said thoughtfully.

"You are the key to our future," Paul said excitedly.

"I am?"

Paul came up to the bed. "I was going to wait, but now is as good a time as any. I have a proposal for you."

"What proposal?"

"I humbly beseech you to allow us to come and live at the Home."

"What?" Joshua, startled, swung his legs over the edge of the bed.

"You heard me." Paul stared into Joshua's eyes.

"Are you serious?"

"Absolutely," Paul stated earnestly.

"But you have lived in the Twin Cities all these years," Joshua pointed out.

"And hated almost every waking minute of our miserable existence."

"But the Home isn't large enough to accommodate all of the First Church members," Joshua objected.

"I've thought of that," Paul responded. "We could enlarge the Home, couldn't we? Erect wooden walls and make a new perimeter? You said the soil is fertile and easy to till, and that game is plentiful. We could become pastoral in our lifestyles, become farmers and hunters and live as your Family lives. We could start a new center for mankind's progress! We could begin a new society, a new culture, and a new hope for mankind!"

Joshua grinned at Paul's bubbling vitality. "You've given this considerable thought."

"Yes, Brother Joshua, I have. What do you say?"

"It isn't up to me," Joshua informed him.

"Oh."

"Don't look so downcast," Joshua said, encouraging him. "The final decision on a matter of this import must come from the entire Family. A vote must be taken, and the Elders must be permitted to express their views."

"What do you think they will say?" Paul asked hopefully.

"I have no way of knowing," Joshua admitted.

Paul, dejected, sat down on the bed. "I was so hopeful," he mumbled.

"You have no reason to be so depressed," Joshua said. "I haven't said no. The Family may agree to the idea."

"You really think so?" Paul brightened.

"We'll never know unless I return to the Home."

"And how will you accomplish that?"

Joshua hesitated. Despite his affinity for Paul, he'd wisely withheld telling about the SEAL. There was always the possibility the First Church of the Nazarene might arbitrarily assume possession of the transport if they became aware of its existence. "I will find a way. But first, I must ascertain if my friends have perished. I must return to the site where the Wacks attacked us."

"I don't know . . ."

"I will not return to the Home until I learn the fate of my comrades," Joshua said. "And you will never have the opportunity to leave the Twin Cities if I do not make it back."

Paul nodded. "We could assist you in finding your friends. My men found you wandering, almost senseless, near dozens of bodies. They were attracted by the ravens circling overhead. We could take you there, and see if there are any clues as to their fate."

Joshua smiled, pleased with his subterfuge. "Would you?"

"Of course. I will arrange for it now. Are you up to the exertion required?"

"I won't have any problem," Joshua stated. "My head is sore, but beyond that, I'm fine."

"Good. You can leave in an hour. There is plenty of daylight left." Paul walked from the room, pausing at the door. "You will take care of yourself? We can't allow anything to happen to you."

"I will take care," Joshua promised.

Paul nodded and left.

Joshua smiled, surprised at himself. He had deliberately deceived a brother, a fellow son of God. What in the world was happening to him? First he'd killed. Now he'd lied. What was next? Would he lust after a woman? But his deception was justified, he mentally noted. And he hadn't lied in every respect. He would go with them to the point where the Wacks had attacked. Then, when an opportunity presented itself, he would sneak away from his escort and find the Porns. It shouldn't be too terribly difficult. If he headed west, and avoided the Wacks, sooner or later he would meet the Porns. He would convince them to take him to their leader, and he would prevail upon this Maggot to arrange a meeting with Paul. It could be done! Paul was too pessimistic. The Porns couldn't be that bad! There had to be a glimmer of decency remaining in their jaded souls, and there was only one way to find out.

Joshua smiled.

Hickok would be pleased. This type of devious action was his forte.

Yes, sir! He was really getting the hang of this Warrior business. Besides, the Spirit would preserve him. What could possibly go wrong?

19

If they didn't kill him soon, the blistering heat would.

Blade tried to avert his eyes from the sun, now directly over his head, at the midday position. Another hot August day was halfway done, another day of baking and sweltering and suffering.

How much longer would they keep him in suspense?

Blade recalled his shock upon awakening after the attack on University Avenue. He had found himself completely naked, tied to four stakes imbedded in the earth, his body spread-eagled, face up. Before him had loomed a large gray structure, six stories in height, with most of the windows broken out, the entire building in disrepair. Twenty feet off the ground, no doubt still intact because it was out of reach, had hung a faded, dirty sign. Some of the letters had been smudged, others missing, but sufficient had remained to inform Blade that he was outside a division of the Minnesota State Hospital, a subbranch called The Minnesota Hospital for the Criminally Insane.

Damn!

For over two days he'd lain there in the open, exposed and vulnerable, waiting for the Wacks to finish him.

Why hadn't they?

A shadow fell across his face and he squinted up, recognizing Clorg, the Wacks' leader, a lumbering mass of solid muscle. Clorg wore tattered rags, and his body reeked. Blade doubted the hulking lunatic had taken a bath in his entire life.

Clorg flashed a toothless grin at Blade. "Big Man hungry? Big Man hungry?"

Blade frowned, angry. Clorg came by several dozen times a day to ask questions, to tease him the way a child would tease an adult. He refused to respond.

Clorg drew back his right foot and kicked Blade in the side.

Blade squirmed, pain spinning his vision, the tight ropes around his wrists and his ankles tearing into his flesh. He wondered if he would lose the use of his extremities. Whoever had tied him to the stakes while he was unconscious had done an excellent job. The rope was so secure, so taut, his circulation was almost cut off. His hands and feet were numb.

"Is thirsty? Is thirsty?" Clorg leaned over the captive, leering.

Blade elected to avoid another blow by answering. "I could use some water," he admitted.

Clorg roared with laughter. "Funny! Funny! Funny!"

If I could just break free, Blade thought, grimacing, I'd throttle your stinking neck!

Another Wack joined them, a weasel of a man with a twitching walk and a missing left ear.

Clorg slapped the newcomer on the arm. "Big Man

wants some water!''

The other man grinned. "Does he now?"

Clorg glared down at Blade. "Fant come soon!" he bellowed. "Won't need water! Won't need food! Be our food!" He ambled away.

"I'm truly sorry about all this," said the weasel.

"You are?" Blade's throat was parched and dry, his tongue swollen. He had to strain to talk.

"Any decent person would be."

Blade smiled, his dehydrated, split lips stretching in agony. "My name is Blade," he offered. "What's yours?"

The man drew himself up and, with a flourish, placed his right hand on his narrow chest. "I, sir, am a tree!"

"What?"

"Can't you tell?" The Wack bent his arms and legs at bizarre angles from his body. "My leaves always give me away."

Blade closed his eyes, sighing, frustrated again. How much longer? Who the hell was Fant? When would he get there? What would happen when he did?

Someone giggled.

Blade looked up. The tree was gone, and he had been replaced by a young woman and a small girl, the child not more than ten or twelve. The woman had long, filthy black hair, and wore green shorts and a blue top. Holes had been cut in the front of the blouse, permitting the woman to stick her nipples out. Her left nipple was partially gone, and there were teeth marks on the visible portion of her breast. The girl had on a brown smock.

"I show you," the woman said to the girl. "Watch me good and I tell you."

"Okay, Mommy," the girl replied.

The mother knelt next to Blade, pulling the girl down beside her.

"This important," the woman stated. She glanced at Blade and grinned.

Blade smiled in return. He tried licking his lips. "Hi. My name is Blade."

The mother hauled off and slapped him across the face. "You shut up!"

Blade could feel blood trickling from his mouth.

The girl reached out and touched a finger to his lips. She raised the finger, covered with blood, and placed it into her mouth.

"Watch!" the mother ordered.

The girl nodded, sucking on her finger.

What in the world did they want? Blade lowered his chin so he could keep an eye on them.

The mother, without warning, grabbed his flaccid penis and held it for the daughter to see.

No!

Blade surged against his bonds, heaving, his muscles bulging, hoping this time the ropes would break.

They didn't.

The woman punched him on the chin, knocking him back to the ground.

Dear Spirit! Don't let them mutilate him!

"See?" The mother pointed at his organ.

The girl nodded, still savoring the blood.

"Man," the woman said, shaking Blade's manhood. "Man." She reached between her legs and touched herself. "Woman."

The girl watched her mother's hand.

"Woman not have sticker," the mother stated. "See?"

The girl removed her finger from her mouth. "I see."

183

"Good."

The girl leaned over, touched Blade, then herself. "Like that?"

"Yes," the mother nodded, releasing Blade's penis.

Blade exhaled a sigh of relief.

"Why, Mommy?" the young girl asked earnestly. "Looks very yucky to me!"

The mother considered the question for a moment, finally smiling. "Feels fun," she said.

"Really?"

"Really." The mother stood, drawing her child up.

Blade didn't like the way the girl was staring at his organ, as if an idea had occurred to her.

"Mommy." The girl grinned at her inspiration. "Wanna keep it."

"What?"

"Want to cut it off and save it," the girl stated. "Show it to friends."

"No," the mother replied, turning away.

The girl stamped her left foot. "Want it, Mommy! Want it!"

The mother glanced over her shoulder at her offspring. "No."

"Want it, Mommmy!" the girl shouted, her face reddening, beginning to throw a tantrum.

"No."

"Yes! Yes! Yes!"

The mother backhanded the daughter across the face. "I say no! Clorg get it! He always do."

The girl fell silent, glaring at Blade.

"Come." The mother walked away, the girl in reluctant tow.

Dear Spirit! It had been close! What did the woman mean, saying Clorg would get it? Blade's mind drifted, focusing on Jenny. How he missed her! If he managed to make it back to the Home, he would never leave again. He'd relish Home life, with Jenny keeping him warm at night, and lots of little ones underfoot to provide some spice for their domestic life. Maybe he'd quit the Warriors. After all, who needed this aggravation? This unwarranted grief? He should never have agreed to this foolish venture in the first place! Why had he let Plato talk him into it?

Wait a minute!

What was the matter with him? A little hardship, a bit of adversity, and he's ready to buckle, to give up every value he's cherished?

Blade concentrated, resisting the negative, defeatist thoughts. His battered condition was starting to take its toll, sapping his strength and his mental equilibrium.

There was a growing commotion around him, an increasing number of voices and movement.

What was going on?

Blade glanced in both directions, surprised to see the Wacks converging into a group, surrounding him on three sides. They had staked him in the center of a grassy area, the grass stunted by the frequent stomping of their feet and the weight of their bodies. This grassy tract was a congregation point, a meeting ground, for the Wacks. During the day, at any given time, no fewer than a dozen would be resting or conversing or be engaged in ridiculous antics on the grass. At night, they went inside the building and left him alone. The first night of his captivity he'd stayed awake the entire night, fearing an animal would creep up on him in the dark and feast on his defenseless body. Inexplicably, he hadn't been attacked. Not a thing had disturbed him then or since, and he continually asked himself why. There had to be a reason. What would keep predators out of this area? Another predator? Or something they dreaded even worse?

The number of Wacks gathering about him grew.

Blade roughly estimated those present at one hundred. Based on the activity he'd seen the past several days, he guessed the total Wack population stood at between one hundred and fifty and two hundred. He hadn't seen this many together at one time before.

Clorg emerged from the crowd, carrying the Commando in his right hand. Six of the Wack men followed him as he came up to Blade and angrily waved the Carbine in Blade's face.

"Not work!" Clorg fumed. "Why?"

Blade wondered where the rest of his arms were. Scattered among the Wacks, no doubt, along with his clothes and moccasins.

Clorg pounded on his chest. "Clorg want to know why?"

"It's jammed," Blade told him.

"What?"

"Jammed."

Clorg gripped the Commando in both hands and stared at the gun, confused. "What is jammed?"

Blade realized there was no use attempting to explain. "It won't work," he answered.

Clorg shook the Commando. "Want it work. Make it work!"

"I can't," Blade said. "Not with my hands tied."

"Make it work!" Clorg roared. He swung the barrel at Blade and pulled the trigger.

Instinctively, Blade tried to twist aside, unable to move because of the ropes.

The Commando was still jammed.

Enraged, Clorg brought the barrel of the Commando down on Blade's injured left thigh, on the arrow wound.

Blade thrashed and squirmed, gritting his teeth,

the pain washing over his brain in successively weaker waves of agony. Damn that crazy bastard!

Clorg smiled, watching Blade writhe. "Serves right!"

The other men were laughing.

"Is time for Fant," Clorg announced, turning to face the assembled Wacks. "Time to call on great one! Time for feed on Big Man!"

The Wacks cheered, clapped, and uttered cries of delight at the prospect of another feed, a subtle frenzy transforming the already insane crowd into demented demons.

Blade, sensing his time was running short, tried to break his bonds again, to no avail. What was happening? What did it all mean?

"Time for food!" Clorg shouted, waving his arms. "We call great one! We call Fant!"

The Wacks were jumping and screaming and spinning and weaving.

"Clorg!" Blade yelled.

Clorg ignored him, staring off into the distance, to the west.

"Clorg!"

Clorg reluctantly glared at Blade. "What you want, Big Man?"

"What is Fant?"

Clorg grinned wickedly. "You see. You see, real soon."

"Is Fant a Wack?" Blade desperately wanted to achieve an understanding of what was coming.

"Fant?" Clorg slowly nodded. "Was once like us. No more."

"He's not a Wack anymore?" Blade asked, perplexed.

Clorg squatted, smiling, in a strangely talkative mood. "Not like peoples now. No. Changed."

"Changed? How do you mean?"

187

"You see. Real soon."

"Is Fant an animal?"

Clorg stood, gazing off. "You see. Fant be hungry. Always is. We give Fant you, then Fant leave us be."

"You're going to give me to Fant?"

Clorg lifted his left hand and tapped his head. "Clorg real smart. We feed you Fant, then Fant not eat any of us. Clorg real smart!"

What was all this about? Blade turned his head and scanned the crowd, perceiving the Wacks had enclosed him on only three sides, the north, the east, and the south. Toward the west was open, allowing an avenue of approach. For what? He could see a building about forty yards away to the west, a two-story structure with a section of the facing wall missing, a gaping hole glaring at him like a giant black eye.

The Wacks had quieted and were staring at the building, at the dark opening.

"Cut me loose," Blade said to Clorg, "and I will fix the gun for you."

"Quiet!" Clorg barked.

"But I can fix the gun!"

Angrily, Clorg spun and kicked Blade in the ribs. "I tell you keep mouth shut!"

Blade fought to catch his breath. His right side was in agony.

Clorg, beaming, raised his arms. "FANT! FANT! FANT!" he began to chant.

The clustered Wacks followed suit.

"FANT! FANT! FANT!"

The Wacks were dropping to their knees, their voices calling out the name in unison.

"FANT! FANT! FANT!"

Over and over and over they repeated their cry.

Blade kept his eyes on that huge hole in the wall.

"FANT! FANT! FANT!"

Something was moving in the building with the hole, something large, a patch of pale motion visible against the black of the cavity.

"FANT! FANT! FANT!"

Blade detected a motion at the edge of the aperture, a sinuous rising and falling.

What the hell was it?

"FANT! FANT! FANT!"

Clorg abruptly bent over Blade, gloating, his breath stale and putrid, his thick lips close to Blade's face.

"FANT! FANT! FANT!"

"Now time is come!" Clorg exclaimed. "You die, Big Man!"

"FANT! FANT! FANT!"

The incessant chant was grating on Blade's nerves.

Clorg glanced down at Blade's sex organ. He smacked his lips, drooling.

"FANT! FANT! FANT!"

"I eat soon too," Clorg said in Blade's right ear. "Clorg hungry. Clorg is after Fant."

Blade, comprehending, furious, drew his head back, then swept his forehead up, smashing it against Clorg's nose, feeling the nasal passages collapse and flatten.

"FANT! FANT! FANT!" the Wacks continued their beckoning appeal, oblivious to the conflict between Clorg and Blade, all eyes nervously fixed on the building to the west, on Fant's lair.

Clorg roared in torment, his right hand covering his shattered nose, blood pouring over his lower face.

"FANT! FANT! FANT!" the Wacks intoned, performing a ritual established over three decades ago. For years they had resigned themselves to

Fant's periodic assaults, too terrified to resist. Finally, it had dawned on one of them, the means to end their torment. All they had to do was keep Fant supplied with fresh meat, and Fant would cease his depredations on them. They hoped.

Clorg stood erect, gawking at the red liquid all over his hand and arm.

Blade struggled against the ropes. His time was running out!

The chanting suddenly stopped, as a petrified hush fell over the Wacks.

Blade gaped at the opening.

Fant was emerging from his den.

Dear Spirit! What was it?

Fant stood in the sunlight, blinking rapidly, surveying the scene ahead, the clustered, reeking, noisy ones, and the new food staked to the ground, ready for the feast.

Blade stared in sheer astonishment. *What, in heaven's name, was it?* Never, not even in his wildest imaginings, would he have envisioned such a deformed monstrosity as now confronted him.

Fant shuffled forward, using its arms and two good legs for support, its third leg dragging on the ground, useless.

The Wacks were all on their feet, moving backward, edging away from the approaching beast.

Except for Clorg. He held his hand in front of his face. "Clorg hurt," he said to himself, fascinated at the sight of his own blood.

No! Blade surged against the ropes again, fiercely wrenching his arms and legs, asserting his strength to the utmost, his veins bulging on his arms and legs, sweat running from every pore. He wasn't going to go out like this, helpless, eaten alive! His face turned bright red from his exertion, his temples throbbing with pain. He ignored the discomfort, pushing his body, forcing his muscles to obey his commands. The increased flow of blood and adrenaline began to restore feeling to his hands and feet.

Blade glanced at Fant, now thirty yards away, the grotesque features in clearer detail, vividly, indelibly etched in his mind.

Fant was at least eight feet in height, and at least partially human. The creature was incredibly muscular, undoubtedly endowed with irresistible power. Fant's skin was ashen, almost white, from a habitual lack of sunshine. Its body was squat and short, out of all proportion to its long arms and legs, and completely naked. Between Fant's two legs dangled a third limb, a stunted appendage, a congenital defect, useless, thin and ungainly. The left side of Fant's chest and face consisted of cracked, brown skin, blistering sores, and oozing pus, the trademark of the mutates. Its mouth was a red slit, the nose narrow and flared, the eyes black pools. Fant was utterly hairless.

What was it, Blade wondered? The product of a deformed human fetus, a new brand of mutate, or both?

"No!" Clorg abruptly bellowed, glaring down at Blade. "You hurt Clorg! You die!" He raised the Commando over his head, gripping it by the barrel with the stock aimed at Blade's head.

Blade shifted as the stock came at him, the wood crashing into the ground an inch from his right ear. Infuriated, Clorg brought the stock down again and again, growling like a wild dog. Blade desperately dodged each blow, knowing it was only a matter of moments before Clorg connected. The stock fell wide as Clorg slipped, the wood brushing Blade's right hand as it thumped against the earth. Without thinking, Blade gripped the stock at the point where it narrowed, holding fast, refusing to release the Commando, to relinquish this last hope.

Clorg tugged and jerked on the Carbine. "Let go!" he shouted. He braced his feet and heaved, throwing his exceptionally strong shoulder muscles into the motion.

At the same instant, the one he'd been waiting for, Blade pulled on the stake, his jaw clenched, his right arm strained to the limit, adding his strength to Clorg's, praying his ploy would be successful.

The combined force yanked the stake clear of the ground, and Blade's right hand was free. He twisted, tugging on his left wrist, feeling the left stake give a little. Grabbing the top of the stake, he wrenched it back and forth, the dirt crumbling around the edges as the stake inched upward. It was almost loose!

"No! You die!" Clorg raised the Carbine over his head, carefully aiming this time, wanting to be sure. He froze as a shadow fell across both men, and he bent his neck and looked up into two evil black eyes. "No!" Senselessly, he spun and struck the creature known as Fant across the left leg.

Blade fell back as the left-hand stake came out of the ground. He leaned down and applied both of his arms to the stake securing his right foot.

"No! Not now!" Clorg shouted at the hideous, spidery Fant. "Go away! Feed later!" Clorg struck Fant a second time.

Fant hissed, revealing pointed fangs, and grabbed Clorg by the neck, lifting him clear off the ground and high into the air. Clorg gasped and gurgled, his legs thrashing.

Blade's right foot jerked free and he immediately turned his attention to the final stake.

The assembled Wacks, thoroughly unnerved and

terrified, broke and ran in all directions, screaming and shrieking.

The last stake was extracted, and Blade frantically tore the stakes from his limbs. He ran to the south, toward the hospital thirty yards away, and glanced back over his shoulder.

Fant had crushed Clorg's neck and dropped the body to the earth. Snarling, the disfigured freak began pounding the corpse with its left fist, pulverizing the remains to a pulp.

The Wacks, searching for places to hide and take cover, were trampling one another in their haste and panic. A crowd of them was jammed together at the hospital entrance.

Blade had reached a paved area in front of the Hospital. He stopped to gather his energy and his breath, an intense spasm lancing his left side. He looked back.

Fant dipped his left hand into the bloody mess at his feet, then stuffed a chunk of flesh into his mouth. He chewed slowly, emitting slurping sounds. The moonish face swung sideways, and Fant spotted the group in front of the hospital. Hissing, Fant charged directly at them, directly at Blade.

20

"I don't like it, pard. They're taking too long!"

"Relax, man. Like I told you, Maggot takes his dear sweet time when he's feedin' that ugly puss of his."

"I'm tired of waiting," Hickok stated, his left ear pressed against the door, listening.

"What's your big rush?" Bear asked. He was squatting on his haunches a few feet away. "They'll come sooner or later."

"I can't afford to wait," Hickok said, frowning.

"Why?"

Hickok stared at Bear. "I've got some friends I need to account for, and nothing better have happened to them."

"Bertha?"

Hickok nodded. "Yep. And three others. I don't know where they are. I don't even know if they're still alive. But I've got to find out. They could be needing my help right this moment."

"So what's your plan now?" Bear inquired.

"You'll take me to where Maggot is eating." Hickok stood.

"Say what?"

"You heard me."

Bear also stood. "You're crazy!"

"You said that before," Hickok reminded him.

"This time I mean it! We can't do it," Bear protested, "because Maggot will be with his flunkies. Maybe twelve of them."

"We go," Hickok announced, and cautiously opened the door. He peered both ways to insure the corridor was clear.

"How you figure you're gonna waste Maggot with all his bodyguards there?"

"I'll think of something," Hickok assured him.

"You sure you ain't a Wack?" Bear demanded.

"If I am," Hickok said, grinning, "what's that make you?"

"What do you mean?"

"You're following me, aren't you?" Hickok eased out the door into the hall.

"Damn!" Bear exclaimed. He hesitated, considering the risks. "Oh, hell!" Smiling, he followed Hickok.

"Where is Maggot right now?" Hickok asked when Bear joined him.

"About three stories up." Bear pointed at the ceiling.

"You know this place," Hickok said. "What's the best way to get to him without anyone seeing us?"

Bear pondered the question. "We're lucky that no one uses this lower level too much. We can take the stairs up to the third floor. There might not be too many using the stairwell."

"Is there any other way?"

"Just the shafts," Bear casually mentioned.

"The shafts?"

"Wait a minute, Hickok," Bear immediately objected. "We can't use the shafts."

"Why not?"

"Why, the only way up them is the cables!"

"The cables?"

"Yeah. They hang down the middle of the shafts. We'd have to climb them. Three stories!"

"Let's go." Hickok beckoned for Bear to lead the way.

"You don't understand," Bear complained.

"Then show me."

Bear shrugged and led Hickok to the right. The corridor was lit by torches attached to the walls at twenty-foot intervals. The door to the pit was at one end of the hallway. In the center were two open doors, revealing two confined chambers, measuring five feet by five feet.

"What the blazes are these?" Hickok asked. They reminded him of two immense closets.

"Beats me," Bear replied. "No one knows what they were used for. Look at those." He pointed at two square openings, one in the roof of each closet. "You can climb up and get on top of these things. That's where the cables are. They're fastened to the middle of the roofs, and they go straight up to the top of this building, which is eight stories high."

"Which reminds me," Hickok said. "Where is this building?"

"Oh. It's on our turf, of course, in pretty safe territory. Think it was called the Riker Manufacturing Complex before the war. Off of Olsen Memorial Highway."

"How far from no-man's-land?" Hickok needed to know.

"From where they found you?"

Hickok nodded.

"About five or six miles."

Hickok sighed. "Let's get this over with." He

entered the left cubicle and glanced at the opening above his head.

"Now just a minute . . ." Bear began.

"Now what's the matter?" Hickok snapped, impatient with Bear's constant carping.

"This ain't such a bright idea," Bear informed him.

"You say it leads to the floor Maggot is on?"

"Sure enough."

"And we won't encounter other Porns using this way?"

Bear grinned. "None of 'em would be loony enough to try it!"

"Good." Hickok leaped, catching the edges of the opening, pulling his body up and through, bracing his feet on either side of the square after attaining the roof.

Bear stepped into the compartment and looked up. "You're goin' to do it?"

"You need to ask?"

"What if the cable breaks?"

"Try and put me back together before you bury me."

"Damn! You sure are one contrary honky!" Bear muttered. He walked around to the other cubicle and followed Hickok's example, pushing his Winchester onto the roof before he clambered on top.

"This is a great idea," Hickok complimented him.

"You think so, huh?" Bear nervously peered into the darkness, uncomfortable, assailed by the oppressive silence and a sensation of being watched. Something rattled to his left. "What was that?" he asked, scooping up his Winchester.

"Just me." Hickok stood and tested the cable, yanking as hard as he could, wondering what it was secured to on high.

"Don't do that!" Bear cried out. "You like to scared me half to death!"

Hickok had already replaced the C.O.P. in the holster strapped to his left leg. The Mitchell's Derringer was firmly attached to his right wrist. Not much, considering the arsenal Maggot had at his disposal and the number of men on his side, but it would have to do. "Are you all set?" he asked Bear.

Bear was bothered by the lack of light, just enough filtering in through the openings to enable him to detect Hickok's form on top of the other cubicle. He gazed up the shaft, noting that black stretches alternated with patches of light at each story. All of the doors to the shaft had been pried open long ago, and the light from the respective hallways provided minimal illumination.

"Are you ready?" Hickok demanded.

"As ready as I'm gonna be."

Hickok gripped the cable and jumped, wrapping his ankles around the cable for added support as he slowly climbed, hand over hand, toward the next story.

Bear tucked his Winchester under his belt, angling the rifle along his right hip. He tightened the belt to insure he wouldn't lose the gun as he scaled the cable.

"Will you come on!" Hickok's voice carried from the darkness above.

Bear took a deep breath, grabbed the cable, and started his ascent, mounting the cable in the same fashion as Hickok. He found himself speculating whether the rats could climb the cable.

Hickok reached the open doors at the first-floor level. He paused, hanging onto the cable, waiting for Bear to catch up.

"Is somethin' wrong?" Bear asked when he

reached a position on his cable directly aligned with Hickok. The two cables were eight feet apart.

"I thought maybe you were taking a nap," Hickok cracked.

"You ain't funny, man," Bear responded.

"I remembered what these things were called," Hickok informed him.

"You do?" Bear spoke softly, his eyes on the portion of the first-floor hall visible through the open doors.

"Yep. They were tagged elevators, I believe."

"Remind me to tell you how impressed I am," Bear said, "after I get off this cable!"

Hickok grinned and resumed ascending his cable, his wrists, already injured in the pit incident, smarting painfully. They had to hold out until he reached the third floor! If he lost his grip now, he'd bust his skull in the fall.

Bear paced his exertions, keeping level with Hickok. He wondered how Hickok and Bertha had met, and he hoped Bertha was still alive because he wanted to see her again, to tell her all the things, express all his feelings, the emotions, he'd never been able to display before she deserted the Porns for the Nomads. Why hadn't he gone with her? She had wanted him to go with her, even pleaded with him, tears in her beautiful eyes. And he'd refused. In all his years, Bear castigated himself, he'd never met a bigger asshole than the person he saw when he stood in front of a mirror.

They reached the second-floor doors and paused, resting.

"Only one more to go," Bear whispered to Hickok.

Hickok nodded and grinned.

The voices and the two women were on them before they could scurry for cover.

"I don't like it one bit," the first woman stated as

they walked into view, engaged in conversation, slowly passing the open elevator doors.

Hickok and Bear hung in plain view, scarcely daring to breathe, waiting to see if the women would spot them.

"I don't like it none either," the second young woman said, "but I don't see what I can do about it."

"I know what you can do," the first woman, a brunette in a faded green dress, commented.

"Like what?"

"Stick a knife in the bastard," suggested the brunette.

"You're nuts!" the second woman, dressed in baggy brown pants and a yellow shirt, exclaimed. "I'd never get away with it."

"Sure you could." The brunette grabbed her friend by the arm and the pair stopped. "You just tell his buddies you found him dead. I'll back you and be your alibi."

"I don't know," the other woman said uncertainly.

"It's the only way you'll get rid of him."

"I know."

"Don't you want me anymore?" the brunette asked.

The second woman kissed the first on the lips. "Of course I do!"

"Then you'll do as I say," the brunette directed.

Her companion nodded and they continued along the hall. Neither of them had glanced into the shaft.

Hickok looked at Bear, who shrugged and led the way up the cables. They slowed as they neared the third floor, cautious, anxious to avoid committing the blunder they'd pulled on the second floor.

"I've never seen any person eat as much as him!" a male voice wafted down the elevator shaft.

"Quiet! Do you want him to hear you?" asked a woman.

"He can't hear me."

"He has ears everywhere!" the scared woman stated.

"This is our fourth trip to the food pots!" protested the man.

"At least we're alive to make the trip," the woman snapped testily.

The sounds of conversation faded.

Hickok inched up the rope until his eyes were above floor level. He leaned out and glanced both ways. "The hall is empty," he whispered to Bear.

"You still sure you want to go through with this?" Bear queried.

"How many times must I tell you?" Hickok replied. "It's time the Porns had a new leader."

"I hope you know what you're doin'."

"So do I."

"You sure can give a man confidence," Bear sarcastically quipped.

Hickok scaled the cable until his feet were above the hall level. He swung his legs forward and back, twice, and on the second swing he vaulted into the corridor, landing crouched, already drawing the C.O.P., scanning for any sign of Porns.

A moment later Bear joined him. He pulled the Winchester from his belt and checked to see if a round was in the chamber. "I'm as ready as I'll ever be," he told Hickok. "Which ain't sayin' much."

The hallway was carpeted and both walls were covered with wood paneling, some of the panels broken or cracked or missing altogether. Torches hung in special brackets on the walls.

"Which room is Maggot in?" Hickok inquired.

Bear waved him to their right, to a closed door ten

feet away.

"This is it," Bear remarked. "The eating room."

Hickok gently twisted the knob and quietly opened the door a foot. He peered around the jamb.

The meal was still in full swing. A table large enough for a dozen diners was in the center of the lavishly decorated chamber. Maggot, like a plump, ponderous hyena presiding over a flock of vultures, sat at the far end of the table on a chair higher than any other. His cheeks and jowls were coated with food and grease. He was smiling as he scooped mouthful after mouthful from a large bowl, using a white ladle, gulping the chunks of food without bothering to chew. Ten other men also sat at the table.

Hickok noted several items of interest. Rat was sitting immediately to the left of Maggot. All of the men were armed, but they had leaned their rifles against the wall behind their respective chairs, and out of their reach. Some of them would be packing handguns, but he wouldn't know which ones for sure until they drew. He did know Rat had the Taurus on his left hip. His eyes lit up when he spotted his Pythons and the Henry, all three on top of the table within Maggot's easy grasp. He eased out to the corridor.

"Are they still in there?" Bear whispered.

Hickok nodded.

"So how do we play this?" Bear inquired.

"You give me your Winchester and take off," Hickok answered.

"Do what?"

"Just give me your gun and get out of here."

"I thought you wanted my help," Bear, taken by surprise by this unforeseen development, noted.

"I did," Hickok concurred. "But I've changed my mind. I'm going in there alone."

"Why?" Bear quizzed. "I don't understand."

Hickok drew Bear away from the door. "Listen, friend." He placed his left hand on Bear's broad shoulders. "One of us needs to stay alive. There's a chance we'd both be blown away if we barged into that room."

"I ain't lettin' you go in there alone," Bear affirmed.

"I've got to."

"No way, Hickok." Bear vigorously shook his head. "I ain't runnin' this time. I'm stickin' by you!"

"Don't do it for me. Do it for Bertha."

"What?"

"Didn't you tell me you and Bertha are friends?"

Bear nodded.

"Good. Then get back to where they found me. That's where I saw her, and my other friends, in that area. If something happens to me, I can go out easier knowing you'll be searching for them and helping them if you find them. Their names are Blade, Geronimo, and Joshua. You'll know them easy enough. They're as crazy as you say I am."

"Was Bertha still alive last you saw her?" Bear asked, his tone tinged with unconcealed concern.

Hickok noticed, his brow creasing. What did this mean? Was Bear more than a friend to Bertha?

"Was she?" Bear gripped Hickok's left arm. "I got to know!"

"She was well when I saw her last," Hickok slowly acknowledged.

Bear breathed an audible sigh of relief.

"I get the impression you like her a lot," Hickok casually offered.

"I guess I do," Bear confessed. "More than I been willing to tell anyone, even her. I've decided to ask her to be mine."

203

Hickok turned away, pretending to watch the door. "Well," he said softly, "I reckon life is plumb full of little surprises."

"What do you mean?"

Hickok faced Bear, a devil-may-care smile on his lips. "I mean, pard, it's more important than ever that you stay alive and find Bertha."

"And you?"

"I got a score to settle with Maggot." Hickok took the Winchester from Bear. "You wait at the end of the hall. If I ain't the one who comes out of this room after all the shooting is done, hightail your butt out of here and go find Bertha and my pards."

"I don't know . . ." Bear said reluctantly.

Hickok gazed into Bear's eyes. "Go, Bear, now." His voice was low and hard.

Bear started to shuffle away. "Is something wrong?"

"What could be wrong?" Hickok walked to the door, his back to Bear. "Get the hell out of here. Now!"

Bear went, unwillingly, confused by Hickok's abrupt change.

Hickok held the C.O.P. in his left hand and raised the Winchester. Good! He could use his thumb and forefinger to grip the rifle barrel and still hold onto the palm gun with his other three fingers. The Winchester contained six shots in its tubular magazine, the C.O.P. four. As a backup, he had his Mitchell's Derringer on his right wrist.

Time to even the score!

He stared at the door, seeing Bertha's face. What was Bear to her? She'd never even mentioned him. Why not? If Bear liked her so much, she had to be aware of his feelings. Maybe Bear was the real reason she had been so dead set against coming back to the Twin Cities? Maybe she felt guilt because she found herself liking both men, one of whom came from a completely different background and culture. What chance did they have? Realistically speaking? They were as different as night and day. Literally. How would the Family react if Bertha and he become involved? What would they say? Since when had he cared what anyone else thought? He shook his head, his blond hair swirling. Enough of this morbid reflection!

Hickok grinned, recalling a statement he'd made to Blade and Geronimo after they'd killed a mutated bear. "I'd rather die in a fight, with my guns in my hands." Wasn't that what he'd said?

Well, now was as good a time as any!

That was when the door opened.

21

The second blow from the tail knocked Geronimo into the putrid pond, the water filling his mouth. He rose to the surface as the creature spun on him, coughing, shaking his head to clear his vision. He grabbed his tomahawks and braced his legs, waiting, his mind racing, trying to identify his attacker.

The beast was at least six feet long, half of it tail. It had four clawed feet, but its main arsenal was the mouth, filled with those razor teeth, some of which protruded from the sides of its jaw.

Geronimo thoroughly enjoyed nature books. He'd read all of the Family books on wildlife, and as the reptile bore down on him, he called to mind two possibilities. An alligator or a crocodile. He didn't know which this was, and the name didn't matter. What counted was the method of dispatching the thing. If his memory served, alligators and crocodiles were tough to kill, tenacious and savage when aroused. And this one was definitely aroused!

The creature was within biting range, the mouth open and targeted on Geronimo.

Geronimo sidestepped, his movements sluggish and slow because of the water. He slashed with his right tomahawk, the edge biting into the side of the reptile's mouth, drawing blood, but causing only a minor wound. He swung his left tomahawk, the blade connecting on top of the creature, above the eyes. The blow stunned the reptile, but the tough skin deflected the blade.

The reptile submerged.

Geronimo twisted and turned, the back of his neck tingling. He couldn't see into the water! The thing could grab him by the leg, pull him under, and drown him! He glanced at the ladder, thirty yards distant, his one hope!

Something brushed against his right leg.

He swam, still grasping his prized tomahawks, his arms and sturdy legs churning the water.

Great Spirit, preserve him!

Geronimo narrowed the distance to the ladder. Maybe the reptile would let him go. Maybe it had attacked him because he had pushed against it. Did alligators or crocodiles eat humans?

The reptilian monstrosity swept out of the water, the head breaking the surface, the jaws clamping onto Geronimo's left leg below the knee.

No!

Geronimo bent and imbedded his left tomahawk in the creature's left eye, the blade buried deep, blood flowing from the gash and spreading, turning the murky water a rust-colored hue.

The reptile went under again, releasing its grip on Geronimo's leg and wrenching the tomahawk from his hand.

Without hesitation, disregarding his hurt leg, Geronimo resumed swimming, his eyes fastened on the ladder.

He was getting close!

Geronimo mentally ticked off the feet remaining, expecting the beast to latch onto him again at any moment. He plowed through the piles of litter in his path, the filth clinging to his clothes and face.

Something nipped at his right foot, but was unable to get a hold on the pumping extremity.

Left arm, right arm. Left arm, right arm. Keep the legs thrashing. Left arm, right arm. He kept his rhythm steady and measured, knowing to panic now was to die.

Another reptile, a smaller version of the first, appeared to his right, lying in the water with its eyes and snout exposed. This one vanished as he drew near.

How many of the things were there? Did they ever attack in groups?

The rungs of the ladder were ten yards from his hands. Eight. Six.

Almost there!

Geronimo reached the metal rungs and gripped the lowest one with his left hand, slipping as he pulled himself up. He grabbed the ladder again and heaved, at the same instant the reptile was on him again, the jaws closing on his right foot.

Great Spirit!

Geronimo brutally brought the right tomahawk down, cutting into the reptile's other eye.

The thing refused to release his right foot.

He swung again, the tomahawk digging a furrow between the eyes. His left hand, still wet, began to loose its hold, and he slipped in the water up to his waist.

Furious, blinded, the reptile freed his foot and sank, agitating the water with its death throes, the blood pouring from its injuries.

Geronimo hastily climbed the ladder, holding fast to the metal rungs, the sunlight hurting his eyes.

Squinting, he managed to reach the circular opening. He squeezed through and rolled to his left, gasping for air, exhausted.

He'd made it!

How long had he been underground? His eyes were stinging and watering like mad. He rested, happy, relishing the fresh air and the warmth from the sun. Never, in all his life, had the sun looked so good as it did now. It was surprising how many blessings you could take for granted.

The pounding of feet alerted him to the fact he wasn't out of danger yet.

Geronimo sat up, finding himself in the middle of a street. Shabby, crumbling buildings lined both sides of the road. Two gutted automobiles were at the curb twenty feet away. An alley intersected the street about ten feet to his right.

The sound of someone running came from the alley.

Geronimo rose to his feet, a bit unsteady. He still had the Arminius in the shoulder holster under his right arm.

Whoever was coming down the alley was making a lot of racket, knocking cans aside and breathing heavily.

Geronimo slipped his solitary tomahawk under his belt and drew the Arminius, the revolver soaking wet. His left leg and right foot were torn and bleeding. They would require attention as soon as he tended to his new business. He was sick and tired of being the victim, of being set upon again and again and again. This time, it would be different. He'd do the attacking for a change of pace!

Another trash can toppled to the pavement.

Geronimo ran to the alley entrance and hid to one side, the Arminius in his left hand. He tensed, ready, estimating the distance, and when a blurred form hurtled from the mouth of the alley, he flicked his left leg out and tripped the newcomer.

"Damn!"

The runner crashed to the pavement, pinwheeling, the sunlight gleaming from bladed weapons.

Geronimo pointed the Arminius at the target, his finger tightening on the trigger.

They weren't getting him this time!

22

The gory fiend was coming in his direction!

Blade reached the hospital entrance, the doorways choked with frantic Wacks, the crazies fighting amongst themselves in their frenzied fear for safety.

"Don't panic!" Blade shouted. "We can all get inside if we don't panic!"

The Wacks totally ignored him, tearing and pulling at one another, each one trying to be next through the doors.

"Calm down!"

A woman in front of him turned and spit in his face.

A man kicked him in the shins.

Blade glared at both of them, his lips compressed, his nostrils flaring. Enraged, he backhanded the man and sent him reeling. He grabbed the woman by the front of her blouse and tossed her aside.

"Move!" he roared, plunging into the crowd, punching and kicking, dispersing those around him, pressing for the doors.

A lean man jumped him from behind and wrapped his skinny arms around Blade's throat. Blade reached up, gripped the Wack by his black hair, and pulled, sweeping the loony over his shoulder and plowing his face into the pavement. Another crazy took a swing, but missed. Blade socked him in the gut, doubling the Wack over. He jammed his right knee into the man's face, and the Wack dropped, clutching his shattered nose, blood covering his hands.

Fant roared, the breeze carrying the scent of the Wacks in front of the hospital directly to its sensitive olfactory organ. Fant slowed, observing the Wacks' pandemonium.

Blade's attention was arrested by a flash of light to his left. One of the Wacks was wearing the Bowies! He also had on Blade's pants. The sunlight glistened from the handles and part of the blades as the long knives bounced in their scabbards. The Wack was engaged in fighting his way to the doors, and he hadn't even remembered to employ the knives!

Blade clasped the man by the right wrist. "Hey, you!"

Snarling, the Wack spun on Blade and lunged at his face. Blade knocked the man's hands down, formed his own right hand into a Tiger Claw, and gouged the Wack in the jugular. The kung fu blow crushed the Wack's windpipe and he gagged and fell to his knees. Blade grabbed the man's head in a steely grip and twisted, sharply, to the right. He heard the spine pop as the vertebra snapped in two.

Blade glanced over his shoulder, afraid Fant was on them.

One of the Wacks, a man braver or more foolish than the rest, had ran in front of the monster. He was jumping up and down and flapping his arms, shouting for Fant to stop.

Which it had. The creature was standing still, the

eyes glaring at the prancing Wack.

The Wacks at the door were still wildly attempting to reach the interior of the building and safety.

Blade crouched and quickly stripped the dead Wack of his pants and the prized Bowies. He hastily checked the right front pocket, fearing the worst, but he was elated to discover the keys still there.

Fant had not moved.

Blade hastily slipped into his pants, relieved at being clothed again. He ran his fingers over the Bowie handles, caressing them, the knives snug in their sheaths against his hips. He felt whole once more. A part of him had returned.

A scream of terror sounded behind him.

Blade whirled, drawing his Bowies.

Fant had bowled the Wack over and stepped on his chest. The Wack sputtered and twitched as blood and froth spewed from his gaping mouth.

Blade tried to move the mob with reason one final time.

"Quit shoving! There's room for all of us if we take our time!"

A fat man pivoted and aimed a club at Blade's face.

"Damn!"

Blade ducked under the blow, grinning, released from any obligation he might have entertained about not hurting these poor, pathetic, mentally deficient slobs, lunatics who could not be held accountable for their actions.

He gutted the fat man.

A woman shrieked.

Blade dove into the mass of crazies, swinging the Bowies with devastating effect, hacking arms and slashing throats and stabbing with reckless abandon.

Behind him, a sinsister, eerie sibilation warned him that Fant was almost on them.

Only two men barred his entrance to the hospital. They were jammed in the doorway, wrestling, striving to be next to enter.

Blade couldn't afford to waste any time. He plunged his knives into their vulnerable backs, one in each man, and shoved, driving them through the doorway and jerking the blades free. They toppled to the tiled floor, writhing, contorted.

The doors to the hospital had once incorporated glass panels, broken decades ago, leaving the metal strip casings attached to hinges, the frames tilting toward the ground.

Blade entered the gloomy interior of the hospital, stepping over the two Wacks, debating his next move. Was there a rear exit to the building? Were there more crazies inside, lurking in the dark, ready to pounce on unsuspecting victims?

An uproar behind him drew his attention.

Fant had plowed into the crowd of Wacks in front of the hospital, scattering the ones able to flee, and pounding on those Blade had left lying on the tarmac. Within a matter of two minutes, Fant was the only creature still standing, the only thing still alive, outside the building entrance. Fant savagely mashed the last body into the pavement, the blood and flesh and bones forming a repulsive pile of mush. It gazed into the hospital, and for a moment Blade thought it might try to enter, although it would have a hard time getting through the doorway. Instead, Fant turned and began feeding on one of the bodies.

A bearded Wack suddenly sprang from the darkness, trying to tackle Blade. Blade sidestepped, backing away, wary, expecting others. The Wack scrambled to his feet, growling, and lunged. Blade brought both knives up and in, burying them in the Wack's chest, holding the crazy at arm's length until he stopped moving, and then dropped him. He turned, scanning for a way out, alert for more adversaries. There had to be more Wacks in the hospital. He just knew it.

From somewhere in the depths of the building came a maniacal laugh.

Damn!

From the frying pan to the fire!

Blade held the Bowies ready at his waist. The tile felt cool on the soles of his naked feet as he padded down the hall. He stopped when the corridor branched in three directions, one branch proceeding straight ahead, the second leading to the left, the third to his right.

Which way to go?

Blade selected the central corridor, telling himself the fastest way between two points is always the straightest. He hoped.

A rustling sounded from the black hallway to his right as he passed it.

Blade treaded cautiously, uneasy. The Wacks hadn't bothered to light the inside of the hospital. Considering their exceptional night vision, they probably didn't need any illumination. But he did, and he had another problem to contend with. The enforced lack of food and water and rest, combined with the beatings and the fights, had taken a terrible toll on his body. He was weak and unsteady, and he couldn't afford prolonged combat in his current condition.

The sooner he got out of this madhouse, the better!

Feet were shuffling along the corridor behind him.

Blade whirled. He could see several moving shadows about ten yards to his rear. They were holding back, waiting for the right moment to strike.

Blade broke into a run, keeping to the center of the hallway, figuring the middle was least likely to be cluttered with obstacles. He passed countless rooms, even darker than the corridor. From some of the rooms came sounds, low moans and groans and sighs, coughing, and in one instance, a scream.

The pursuit was picking up.

His legs were balking at the sustained pace, cramps lancing his calves and thighs, the arrow wound throbbing.

Damn!

Where was an exit? There had to be some! How long was this mental hospital, anyway?

A swath of sunlight ahead gave him hope.

Thank the Spirit! Maybe it was an exit.

It was, the door in the same condition as the front entrance.

Blade bolted through the doorway and onto a parking lot, devoid of vehicles, littered with trash and debris. He stopped and doubled over, his lungs heaving, the strain taking its toll.

That was when the Wacks hit him.

They piled out of the doorway, four men, each armed, and tackled him before he could defend himself.

Blade spun as they struck him, one of them pinning his legs, another grabbing him around the waist, the other two going for his arms, attempting to clasp them and restrain him. The loony on his left managed to grip his wrist, but the one on his right missed, and as they went down in a tumbling heap the Wack clutching his abdomen bit his stomach, tearing the flesh, ripping the skin from his body and gulping the morsel down his throat.

Furious, Blade lunged with his right Bowie, the

point of the blade piercing the throat of the Wack on his right and drawing a flow of blood, continuing to sweep the knife in a smooth arc, burying the Bowie in the neck of the crazy holding his left wrist. The man screeched and released his arms, leaping to his feet and pressing his hands against the hole in his neck.

Don't stop! Keep calm!

Blade reversed both knives, sweeping the Bowies in and imbedding them in the neck of the Wack chewing on his stomach, the blades slicing the neck in half. The man convulsed as his blood poured over Blade's chest and belly. Blade heaved, dislodging the Wack, concentrating on the one holding his legs.

The Wack let go and jumped up, an axe in his left hand.

Blade rolled as the loony brought the axe down, the handle brushing his left shoulder. He lunged to his feet and stood braced, his heart pounding in his chest.

He couldn't take much more of this!

One of the Wacks was dead, the one who'd tried to eat him alive. The other two were seriously injured, and one of them ran into the hospital, screaming.

Damn! Reinforcements would be coming soon! He had to end this, now!

The Wack wielding the axe was playing it safe, staying out of Blade's reach, biding time until help arrived.

This was getting him nowhere!

Voices were raised in alarm in the building.

Time for a desperate move!

Blade tried a basic knife-fighter's ploy, feinting with his left Bowie, slashing at the Wack and causing him to bound to one side to avoid the blow. The man was off guard and off balance in the second it took him to move, and in that instant Blade drew his right arm back behind his ear and flung the Bowie with all his might, the knife clearing the four feet between them and sticking into the Wack's chest above the left breast.

The man's eyes bulged and he wildly tugged at the Bowie, withdrawing several inches of the blade before he collapsed on the pavement.

Blade wrenched his knife loose, and ran, bearing for the far end of the parking lot, avoiding the ruts and cracks in the aged tarmac. His lungs were hurting, and he had to limp, the wound on his left thigh open again and bleeding profusely. He reached the edge of the parking lot and paused, glancing back, his breathing labored.

Damn!

A score of Wacks were outside the rear exit, standing around the men he'd cut. One of the crazies, a woman, spotted him.

"There he go! After him!"

Yelling and screaming in anticipation of their next meal, they came after him.

Blade pivoted and hurried along the street bordering the parking lot, searching for a hiding place or a suitable position to make a stand. Not that he entertained any delusions about his ability to withstand another onslaught. If they caught up with him now, he was as good as dead.

He reached an intersection and bore right, frantically seeking any cover.

The Wacks were out of sight, coming up the street from the parking lot, still a distance from the intersection.

Blade slowed as he neared a ruined automobile. The hood and all four doors were gone, and the inside had been set afire, the seats a charred wreck. The tires were gone, but the body was supported on cinder blocks.

Cinder blocks?

Had someone placed the car on the blocks for a purpose?

Blade stopped and knelt. There was a foot of space between the floor of the car and the ground. It would be a tight fit, but it was his best hope! He lay on his back and quickly pulled himself under the automobile, out of sight.

The Wacks reached the intersection, and there was momentary confusion as they argued over which direction their prey had taken.

"This way!" a man shouted. "Me saw him go this way!"

They poured down the street Blade had selected.

Blade held his breath, his body tense, considering the merits of his move. If they found him now, he wouldn't have room to move, to fight back.

A moot point.

The Wacks came alongside the destroyed vehicle, and kept running.

Blade twisted his neck and watched the dirty feet pound the pavement, racing away from his hiding place. He craned his head out from under the car.

The Wacks reached the end of the block and paused at another intersection.

"This way!" a woman yelled. "This way!"

As one, they made off to the left, disappearing from view, the sound of their cries fading.

Blade wearily clambered from under the vehicle and stood on shaky legs. He required rest and nourishment, but where would he find it in the Twin Cities? Everyone he met would be a potential enemy, prepared to kill him on sight.

A wave of dizziness struck him and he leaned against the car for support, breathing deeply until the sensation passed.

Blade noticed an alley ten feet away and he

shuffled into it. Maybe he could locate a secluded spot where he could lay down and sleep for a spell.

The alley was packed with old, rusted trash cans, broken furniture, and other articles.

Blade weaved between the obstructions, forging ahead.

Loud cries abruptly broke the silence behind him.

Had the Wacks returned?

Blade worriedly glanced over his right shoulder. He couldn't see any of the crazies, but they might have returned, backtracking, realizing he had given them the slip.

He had to hide!

Blade stumbled forward, bumping into a trash can and knocking it over, creating a racket, but not caring anymore. He was too tired, and depressed. He'd failed. Failed miserably. Failed Plato, and he hit another can, and Jenny, and he was picking up momentum, and Hickok, and he kicked another can out of his path, and Joshua, and . . .

He saw the end of the alley coming up, and he ran, drawing his Bowies in case they were waiting for him, catching a glimpse of a leg suddenly poking out and tripping him, and his vision spun as he went down, hard, knowing the Wacks had caught him and determined to give them an accounting they would recall for generations to come.

Blade scrambled to his feet, surprised to discover the business end of a revolver staring him in the face.

"Blade?"

It took Blade a moment to recognize the man standing in front of him. He was covered with sewage and filth and grime, his skin almost black from the dirt.

"Geronimo?" Blade asked incredulously.

"Blade! It's you!" Geronimo impetuously embraced his friend, hugging him close.

Blade returned the affection. "I can't believe it," he mumbled.

"Believe it!" Geronimo elatedly exclaimed.

Blade held Geronimo at arm's length, and stared into his eyes. "I've never been so happy to see anyone in my whole life."

"The feeling is mutual." Geronimo's brown eyes twinkled. "Where have you been? I thought the Wacks had you."

The Wacks!

"It's a long story." Blade glanced at the alley. "Right now we've got to get the hell out of here or we'll wind up being the prime rib on someone's plate!"

"Are they after you?"

"Yeah. And I don't mind telling you, I'm running out of steam."

"Don't worry," Geronimo assured him, smiling, the white of his teeth a stark contrast to the smudged dirt all over his face. "We'll get out of this mess in one piece."

"I hope," Blade stated as they jogged away from the alley, "the same can be said for Hickok, Joshua, and Bertha."

"You and me both!"

23

Hickok raised the C.O.P. and blasted the shocked Porn in the face, the man tumbling backward from the door he'd just opened and collapsing on the floor.

The men at the table froze, some with their spoons or forks in midair.

Hickok knew he couldn't afford to miss a beat. He rushed into the dining room, the Winchester already at his shoulder. By all rights, and his Warrior training, he should have gone for the men nearest him, the ones posing the immediate threat, but he picked another target, the big gun booming and the slug ripping into Maggot's right shoulder and propelling the fat man from his chair. Hickok went after Maggot for two reasons, two personal justifications, violating every precept of his long and arduous instruction and discipline. First, he wanted Maggot away from the Pythons and the Henry. Secondly, and an overwhelming sentiment, he hated the son of a bitch!

The Porns began to recover from their initial astonishment, some reaching for revolvers, others trying to get to their rifles stacked against the wall.

Hickok swiveled, firing twice, downing the two men to the right of Maggot's chair.

A grizzled Porn on the left side of the table had cleared leather and was pointing a pistol in Hickok's general direction.

The Winchester blew the top of his head off.

A bullet whined by Hickok's right ear.

Hickok spun, snapping a shot at a man who had reached his rifle, catching the man in the head as he gripped his gun.

Another bullet buzzed by Hickok.

Where? He spotted Rat at the far end of the table, crouched behind it for cover, firing.

A burly Porn, one of those closest to the door, decided the best defense was a good offense. His rifle was out of reach, so he lowered his head and charged.

Hickok sidestepped, another slug missing him as he did. He emptied the Winchester, the sixth shot smacking into a Porn's chest and flipping him over.

The burly Porn returned, grappling for Hickok, attempting to confine his arms.

Hickok dropped the Winchester and brought the C.O.P. up.

Rat popped out from under the table and quickly fired, the bullet catching the burly Porn in the left cheek as the Porn pivoted for a better position. The man clutched the side of his face, his eyes rolled, and he fell.

A tall Porn brought an automatic into play, the gun booming, the slug tearing a furrow along Hickok's left side.

Hickok flinched, steadied his hand, and let the Porn have a bullet in the brain from the C.O.P.

Only two Porns remained. Rat cowered at the far end of the table, under cover. The final Porn, a young kid still in his teens, had turned to ice when the shooting erupted, fear immobilizing him, his right hand inches from the revolver he wore on his right hip.

Now, in the momentary lull, the kid came to life, his hand going for the revolver.

"Don't do it!" Hickok tried to warn him.

No good.

The kid drew, the gun barely out of the holster when Hickok shot him in the right eye.

Hickok crouched, searching for Rat. Where was he? Still under the table? Cautiously, holding the C.O.P. in front of him, he bent and peered under the table, finding a maze of chair legs and table legs.

But no Rat.

Hickok stood and walked to his left, stepping over the bodies, puzzled. The table and chairs were the only furniture in the room. Where could Rat be?

He reached the far end of the dining table, speedily placing the C.O.P. on the wood and retrieving his Pythons. The instant the Colts were in his hands, the pearl handles snug in his palms, he felt renewed confidence surge through him.

Hickok glanced down at the floor, at the spot where Maggot's body should be.

Only it wasn't.

What the hell?

A faint scraping came from his left, and he whirled, the Colts cocked and ready.

In the corner of the room, hidden in shadow, twenty feet from the nearest torch, was a door.

So!

Hickok warily crossed to the door, noting it was open a crack.

Distinctly, from the other side of the door, sounded the click of a hammer being drawn back.

Hickok grinned.

Someone is in for a big surprise, he mentally noted. He blasted at the center of the door, four times in rapid succession.

The wood splintered as the slugs penetrated, and someone screamed and dropped to the floor.

Hickok stepped to the door and kicked it open with his right foot.

Maggot was lying on the floor, clutching his stomach, wheezing. A sawed-off shotgun was on the floor too, at his feet.

Hickok pushed the shotgun aside with his left foot.

The room was lit by a solitary torch, and at the opposite side was another door. Open.

No sign of Rat.

"So, ugly." Hickok glared at Maggot. "We meet again."

Maggot coughed, doubling over.

"I wouldn't have thought a few more ounces would hurt that big tummy of yours," Hickok spitefully remarked.

Maggot gazed up at Hickok, his eyes pools of malevolence.

"Yes, well," Hickok said gruffly. "We've got some business to attend to."

"You've killed me, you bastard!" Maggot croaked.

"Not yet, I haven't," Hickok replied. "Who knows? You could even live. I read about a man named Thomas Coleman Younger once. He was called Cole Younger, to those who knew him, and he was shot eleven times during the course of an aborted bank robbery. Eleven times! Imagine that! And, the remarkable thing is, he lived to tell about it. So don't play possum with me, you miserable cur. On your feet! Now!"

Maggot refused to budge.

Hickok leaned over and pressed the barrel of his left Colt against Maggot's chin. "Make up your mind, blubber ass. I haven't got all day. Some of your pards might show up at any moment, and I can't wait until you're in the mood." His voice lowered, harsh and grating. "It makes no nevermind to me which way you go out. I ain't in a charitable mood, but if you want me to splatter your brains right here and now, I'd be happy to oblige."

Maggot's lips trembled as he forced his massive bulk to rise. He stood on his thick legs, weaving, blood oozing from his wounds.

"Good," Hickok said. "Now we're taking a stroll. You go first. Keep your hands on your gut. If you move them, I'll add another asshole to your anatomy!"

Maggot complied, shuffling out to the corridor.

Hickok glanced in both directions before stepping into the hall.

Bear was at one end, nervously pacing. At the sight of Hickok, he smiled and ran up the hall.

"You did it!" Bear exclaimed, overjoyed, scarcely believing his eyes. "You did it!"

"All except for Rat," Hickok stated.

"Aww, don't worry about him! He's probably hiding in a closet right this minute. Without his boss, Rat ain't any danger whatsoever."

"What about the rest of his bodyguards?" Hickok jerked his right Colt toward Maggot.

"There's only two or three others," Bear cheerfully responded. "They ain't likely to give you any trouble once word of this gets out."

"And the Porns?"

"Here comes your answer." Bear pointed.

Doors at both ends of the hall had opened and Porns were pouring into the corridor. Some carried clubs and knives and other weapons, but none possessed a firearm. They slowed as they approached, then stopped, their babble of voices silenced by the sight of their leader, their despised and feared head, barely able to stand on his own two feet.

"What the hell is going on?" a man asked.

"What was all the shooting about?" added a woman.

"Maggot ain't the boss anymore!" Bear announced.

"Oh? Who the hell is?" another man snapped.

"He is!" Bear beamed and pointed at Hickok.

"No, I'm not," Hickok said quietly.

"What?"

"You heard me. I'm not your new leader."

"But you got to be!" Bear objected. "You've beaten Maggot! You're our new head!"

"Are you, or aren't you, mister?" a woman inquired.

Hickok moved forward and paused, staring at both groups of Porns. "Listen to me! I'm not much good with words, but I've got some that need to be said."

"I never disagree with a man holding two revolvers," a young woman mentioned.

"I'm told many of you don't care for this scumbag," Hickok said, indicating Maggot.

"You got that right!" shouted a man.

"The bastard killed my son!" yelled another.

"And my daughter!" hollered a third.

"Then you shouldn't be too upset when I tell you he's resigning his post, effective immediately," Hickok declared.

"What'd he mean by them big words?" one woman whispered to her male companion.

"He said Maggot's ass is grass," the man answered.

"None of you know me," Hickok continued. "I'm not from the Twins. I've seen the way you live, and it sucks! I've heard many of you feel the same way."

The Porns were silently digesting every word.

"Do you want to change the way things are?" Hickok swept them all with his intense gaze. "You don't have to live like animals, never knowing if you'll live through the day! There is hope! There's always hope! And I'm here to offer it to you. The people in the place where I come from might be willing to help you, but only if you're willing to help yourselves. We won't do it all for you! Spread the word! Talk it over amongst yourselves! Make up your minds. Get all the Porns together and take a vote. I'll stick around a while longer, until I hear from your new leader on your decision."

"Our new leader? I thought you said you wouldn't be our head," a man noted.

"I'm not your new leader," Hickok repeated.

"Then who the hell is?" a woman demanded.

Grinning from ear to ear, Hickok turned and faced Bear.

It took Bear a moment to get the message, his eyes widening when he did. "Now wait a minute..." he started to protest.

Hickok raised his right arm over Bear's head. "Say hello to your new leader!" he shouted.

"You crazy motherfucker!" was all Bear could think of to say.

24

Four Porns escorted him into a vast chamber on the first floor of the Riker Manufacturing Complex. The room was packed with over a hundred excited Porns. In the center of the north wall, on a salvaged, cushioned chair, sat a huge black, a Winchester on his lap. Six armed men stood nearby.

The escort stopped five yards from the chair.

"This is the one," the patrol chief announced. "We found him this morning. Said he had to talk with the leader of the Porns."

Bear studied the newcomer. He wore black clothes, the traditional garb of the Horns. His brown hair was worn long, and he covered his face with a full beard.

"Now why would a Horn want to see me?" Bear asked, suspecting a trick. Possibly the honky was a Horn assassin. "Did you check him for weapons?" he quickly demanded of the patrol chief.

"Sure did, Bear."

The newcomer stepped forward, smiling. "Greetings, Brother Bear. My name is Joshua, and I bring a message from Reverend Paul."

229

"Say what?"

"Before I go any further, I should elaborate," Joshua said. "Despite my appearance, I am not a Horn. I come from another place . . . ." Joshua stopped short, startled, as the black leaped from the chair and grabbed him by the front of his shirt.

"Wait a minute! What'd you say your name was?" Bear anxiously queried.

"My cognomen is Joshua."

"But is that your name?"

"One and the same." Joshua grinned.

"And you're from the Home?"

Joshua, surprised, drew back. "How did you know that?"

"Ain't you a friend of Hickok?"

"Hickok!"

"Yeah. Don't you know him? Ain't you one of his pards he keeps talkin' about?"

Joshua gripped Bear's shoulders. "Hickok is here?" he asked, his face lighting up.

"He sure is," Bear replied. "He's restin' right now, and recovering from his wounds."

"Is he hurt?" Joshua demanded, his concern flaring.

"Hey, take it easy, Joshua! You're hurtin' my shoulders." Bear pried loose from Joshua's hold.

"Is he okay?"

"Oh, he's doin' all right," Bear stated. "He was shot and jumped by rats and beat on, and he even managed to get pissed on, but, 'cept for that, he's just fine."

"Where is he?" Joshua eagerly scanned the chamber.

"He's in another room, sleepin'. Don't you worry none," Bear assured Joshua. "We ain't about to let anything happen to him. Hickok is the best thing that's happened to the Porns since who knows when!"

"You sound as if you really care for him," Joshua observed.

Bear smiled, nodding. "I do. He's the one who got me here, as head of the Porns. If the old head, Maggot, was still kickin', you'd be dead right now."

"What happened to Maggot?" Joshua inquired. "I was told he was in charge here."

"Who told you that?"

"Reverend Paul."

"Ahhh. Well, Reverend Paul ain't up on the latest. Maggot is dead."

"Did Hickok kill him?"

Bear chuckled at the memory. "Sure did. He marched Maggot down to this pit under the building and made him stand on a beam for a while, drippin' his blood into the pit." Bear laughed.

"I don't understand," Joshua confessed. "He bled to death?"

"No. No, man." Bear contained his mirth with difficulty. "After a while, see, after the pit was filled with 'em, with hundreds and hundreds of the bastards, attracted by all the blood, Hickok gave Maggot a little shove and down he went. Right into the middle of 'em."

"The middle of what?" Joshua still didn't comprehend.

"Rats, man. Hundreds and hundreds of rats. They've probably cleaned him to the bone by now."

"Hickok did that?" Joshua asked, horrified.

"Yeah. And you know what?" Bear leaned over, lowering his voice confidentially. "I think Hickok enjoyed it. He stood by the pit for the longest time, watchin' them rats eat Maggot."

Joshua shuddered simply imagining the scene.

"Yeah, I know." Bear noticed the tremor. "I couldn't stand to look at it either. The way Maggot was screamin' and beggin' for mercy and all. Pitiful."

"Have you seen my other friends?" Joshua thought to ask, to change the gruesome subject. "Blade, Geronimo, or Bertha?"

Bear shook his head. "Nope. We haven't, and all the Porns been told to be on the lookout for them." He draped his right arm across Joshua's shoulders. "Now what's this message you've got?"

25

Armed messengers, bearing white flags, shuttled among the three factions, exchanging proposals and counterproposals, and two days later a consensus was reached. A momentous summit meeting of the leaders of the Porns, the Horns, and the Nomads would be held at noon the next day in Nomad territory. Nomad turf was selected for several reasons. The general animosity between the Porns and the Horns, a century of accumulated hatred, might erupt into violence if either side ventured onto the other's turf. The leaders pledged the meeting would be conducted peacefully, but they entertained reservations about the self-control of some of their followers. No-man's-land was out of the question, simply too dangerous. The Wacks weren't invited, the prevalent belief being it would be a waste of time, not to mention the certain loss of a messenger, if an invitation were extended to the crazies. The only area remaining was Nomad turf, the ideal choice. The Nomads were comprised of former Horns and Porns, all tired of the incessant fighting, all eager for an end to the hostilities. The Nomads were particularly receptive to the summit conference, and Zahner guaranteed the safety of all parties concerned. The Nomads had established a summer camp on the eastern shore of Moore Lake, comprised of crude huts and makeshift tents. This camp was picked as the summit site.

At noon, under the rules previously agreed upon, each leader, accompanied by two cohorts, climbed a grassy knoll in the center of the camp. Guards were posted around the perimeter of the knoll to insure privacy and prevent any attacks. At the top of the knoll, under the bright sun and blue sky, four wooden benches were positioned in the shape of a square. The Nomads, Zahner and two associates, sat on the eastern bench. The Porns, Bear and two friends, occupied the southern bench. Reverend Paul and two brothers of the First Church of the Nazarene, all three attired in the black apparel customary for the Horns, sat down on the western bench. Joshua and Hickok, as the outsiders and the mediators, used the bench on the north side of the square.

As they were taking their places, Zahner approached Hickok and offered his hand.

"Hello." Zahner smiled. "I'm pleased to meet you. You must be Hickok. Your party arrived only an hour ago, and I've been too busy with preparations to properly introduce myself."

Hickok shook, sizing the Nomad leader up, liking what he saw. A man of integrity, of confidence, reflected in the unwavering blue eyes. "And you're called Z," Hickok stated. "Someone pointed you out to me earlier."

"I've heard a lot about you," Zahner said.

"Oh?"

"Yes. One of the messengers told us about the

gunfight. He said you killed twenty men," Zahner remarked.

Hickok grinned sheepishly. "Only nine."

"Only?" Zahner nodded slowly, impressed. "I've also heard a lot about you from someone else."

"Really? Who?"

"Bertha."

Hickok quickly glanced at Bear, who was sitting on his bench talking with another Porn. He hadn't heard Zahner's statement.

"Bertha is here?" Hickok inquired casually, suppressing his excitement at learning she was apparently safe.

"Yes." Zahner eyed Hickok quizzically. He turned and pointed at a tent fifty yards to the east. "She's in there, and she said she would like to see you as soon as you had the chance."

"Thanks. I reckon I'll see her when I get around to it."

Zahner's brow furrowed, and he shrugged. "Whatever is best. I look forward to talking with you later myself."

"You got it," Hickok promised him, sitting down.

Zahner nodded once and took his seat.

Joshua was the only one still standing. He stood in the center of the square, smiling broadly.

"I want to extend my heartfelt gratitude to each of you," Joshua began his presentation, "for having the courage and wisdom to attend this historic meeting. You have accorded us the singular honor of being your mediators." He indicated Hickok with a wave of his hand. "My brother has expressed his wish that I conduct this conference and do most of the talking. The gift of gab comes naturally to me anyway, so I agreed." Joshua grinned at his joke, then hastily continued when none of the others smiled. "We'll get right to the point for being here. All three of you have expressed a desire to terminate your friction, your warfare, a sentiment shared by the majority of your followers. And who can blame you for wanting peace? For craving a better life? Your entire lives are one continous struggle for existence from the day you are born until the day you pass on. I can only imagine how this brutal environment must affect you, how it must harden you and inhibit you from enjoying the happy, harmonious life that is your birthright as a child of our loving Creator."

Reverend Paul and Bear listened attentively, nodding in agreement at times. They had already covered this topic with Joshua several times. To Zahner, who had not spoken with Joshua before this minute, the experience was a revelation. He hung on every word, amazed.

"You've allowed yourselves to become trapped in a rut," Joshua was saying. "Your lives are dictated by the forces and circumstances surrounding you, instead of you forging the life you want to pursue. You've permitted the hatred of two men, men who lived one hundred years ago, to be perpetuated in your lifetimes. Like a poisonous snake, this hatred has wound down through the decades, destroying countless lives with its toxic bite. How much longer must this insanity be perpetuated? I say it should end now, today! Let there be an end to the senseless bloodshed! Take your destiny in your own hands! Forge a new alliance, a bond of mutual respect and brotherly sharing. Together, you could alter the course of history." Joshua paused, waiting for a response.

"Nice words," Bear finally said. "But I ain't too high on words. Action speaks louder than words."

"I agree with you in principle," Reverend Paul

somberly intoned. "But how do you propose to achieve your goal? How can we change the way things are?"

"I have some ideas," Joshua responded.

"And so do I," Zahner interjected. "There is only one way we can get out of the rut you mentioned, and that's to get out of the Twins. I've heard about the place you come from, this Home as you call it. Why can't you take us there? We could build our new lives with your assistance."

Reverend Paul glanced at Zahner. "You surprise me!" he declared. "I've already made the same recommendation." He grinned in appreciation. "But then, you always were my star pupil."

"What about it?" Zahner pressed Joshua. "Can we come live with you?"

"He told me it isn't feasible," Reverend Paul threw in.

Joshua held up his hands, quieting them. "At this point in time," he emphasized, "it isn't practical."

"Why isn't it?" Zahner questioned.

Joshua sighed. "I would that it were possible, but preparations must be made before an exodus as large as the one you contemplate can be realized. Given time, you could evacuate the Twin Cities, if you wanted."

"No jive?" came from Bear. "All of us could just waltz out of this dive? All of us? There must be . . ." He stopped, calculating.

"Upwards of twelve hundred," Joshua stated. "So you can see why my Family would require time to prepare for your coming. The Home, as it is, is not large enough to accommodate all of you. Your coming would change the Home from a small commune to a town, virtually overnight. Give us ample time to prepare. We can erect wooden walls or a large fence, as Brother Paul has suggested. We'll construct temporary shelters for you to live in until permanent structures can be erected. The Family can also stockpile food so there is ample on hand when you arrive. And remember." Joshua swept them with his gaze. "This journey is hundreds of miles in length, and women and children will be along. What will you do for food along the way? How many miles do you think you can travel daily? You couldn't make the trip in winter. Few of you would survive. You could, however, make the journey in warm weather."

"What's your idea?" Bear asked.

"I have several." Joshua glanced at Hickok for any additional comment, but the morose gunman was staring off to the east, his left elbow on his knee, his chin in his hand. "Hickok and I will return to the Home and present this idea to our Family. They will vote on it, and their decision will be final."

"How will you get back to the Home?" Reverend Paul inquired. "It's a long way to travel for just two men."

"We'll make it," Joshua replied.

Zahner grinned. Bertha had told him about the SEAL. If the outsiders wanted to keep their vehicle a secret, that was their business.

"Do you think your people will go along with it?" Bear asked hopefully.

"I honestly don't know," Joshua answered. "I predict they will."

"What do you think?" Bear queried Hickok.

Hickok sat still, staring at the tent housing Bertha.

"Hey, Hickok!" Bear called. "You still with us or what?"

"What?" Hickok twisted, surprised. "Sorry. I was thinking about something. What did you say?"

"I want to know," Bear repeated, "if you think

your people will go for the idea of all of us coming to live with you?"

Hickok stood and stretched. "I reckon they might. Even if they don't, we'll come up with a better place for you to live than the Twins. There are some small towns not far from the Home, and they might be suitable for our purposes. Don't worry, pard. The Family will back you one hundred percent in whatever you decide to do."

"What about the Watchers?" Zahner asked.

Hickok patted the Colts in his holsters. "We know how to handle them varmits. Besides, how are they going to stop over a thousand people?"

"And what about the Uglies?" Bear threw in.

Hickok picked up his Henry from the bench. "The Family can provide a Warrior escort, and we'll take care of the mutates."

"I'm actually beginning to believe it's possible," Zahner said, astounded. "I thought it was a pipe dream at first."

"I'll leave you boys to work out the details," Hickok informed them. "I've got an errand to attend to right now."

"Where are you going?" Joshua inquired as Hickok strolled off.

"Got something to attend to, pard."

"He sure is actin' strange," Bear commented.

"It's normal for him," Joshua observed. He turned back to the others. "So here is what I propose," he told them. "First, take a vote of your respective groups and determine if they agree on the relocation."

"We don't need to vote," Reverend Paul interrupted. "My brethren will do whatever I tell them to do."

"A vote wouldn't hurt," Joshua tactfully offered.

"Maybe," Paul replied, unwilling to commit

himself.

Joshua shrugged, deciding if he pressed the point, forced Paul to agree to a vote, contention might result. "If everyone accepts the move, begin your preparations."

"Like what?" Bear asked.

"Store what food you can for the journey. Make packs for carrying extra clothes and tools and books and whatever else you want to take along. When you leave the Twin Cities, it might be forever. Whatever you can reasonably take along, take, just so it won't slow you down."

"When do you think we could leave?" Zahner brought up the question uppermost on their minds.

"If all goes well," Joshua answered, "and the Spirit guides us in wisdom and understanding, you could conceivably depart the Twin Cities in late spring or early summer of next year."

"That long off?" Bear complained.

"We couldn't possibly be ready before then," Joshua explained. "And as I noted earlier, you couldn't make the trip in the winter."

"Out of the Twins," Zahner said to himself, realizing the feelings Bertha must have felt. No wonder she had refused to return.

"Is there anything we haven't covered?" Joshua queried them.

"How soon will you return with news of the Family's decision?" Reverend Paul wanted to know.

"Give us a month."

"You won't run out on us?" Bear demanded.

"Do you believe Hickok would run out on you?" Joshua retorted.

Bear grinned. "No way. If he says he's gonna do somethin', then it's as good as done."

"I have another suggestion to make," Joshua said slowly.

"What?" Zahner asked.

"Impose a truce between yourselves. Cease the foolish fighting. Try and work together to prepare for the march to the Home. I know what I am asking is not easy for you, but I pray you will give it a try."

"It will be difficult," Reverend Paul admitted. "But not impossible. If I lay down the law, my brethren will comply."

"The Nomads are more democratic," Zahner commented acidly. "Still, all of us are committed to achieving peace. I don't anticipate any trouble in our camp."

"How about you, Bear?" Joshua faced him.

"Some of the Porns might not like the idea too much," Bear conceded.

"How will you handle them?"

"Easy." Bear grinned. "I'll just tell 'em that whoever don't like the idea can take it up with Hickok."

26

She was patiently waiting for him, sitting up on the cot, propped against three pillows.

Hickok pushed the tent flap aside and entered. "Hello, Black Beauty," he said softly.

"Don't just stand there, White Meat!" She motioned with her left arm, her right side still swathed in bandages. "Come over here!"

Hickok complied, stopping next to the cot.

"Don't I get a hug?" Bertha baited him. "I missed you, honky!" She reached up and pulled him down to the cot, pressing him close with her good arm. He responded, but she sensed an aloof coolness about him, his embrace light and constrained. "Is somethin' the matter?" she asked as he drew back.

"What could be the matter?" Hickok placed the Henry on the ground.

"I don't know," she answered uncertainly. Something *was* wrong, but what? Why was he acting so cold? Hadn't he missed her the way she had missed him?

"I'm happy you're okay," Hickok stated quietly, smiling.

"I thought you were dead," she informed him. "I hear that Joshua is alive too. What about Blade and Geronimo?"

Hickok looked down and sadly shook his head.

"I'm really sorry," she soothed him. "I know how much those two meant to you."

"They were my best pards." His voice was choked with sorrow.

"What's goin' on out there?" Bertha quickly changed the subject.

"They're making plans to evacuate the Twins."

"Really?"

"Yep. They all want to come and live with us, just like you did."

"Like I still do," she corrected him. "I'm lookin' to set up house with a crazy bastard I know." She noticed he didn't grin, and her blood raced. What the hell was wrong? What had she done? Had he found someone else?

"How was it with the Porns?" she questioned him. "I hear you killed thirty of them in a gunfight."

"Not quite," Hickok replied.

"Meet any good-lookin' foxes?" she joked, laughing, except in her eyes.

"Nope."

"You feelin' okay?"

"Yep. I was bruised a bit, and I had to take a bath . . ."

"Had to?"

"Don't ask. Beyond that, it wasn't any big deal. How are you holding up?" He gently touched her bandaged side.

"They tell me I can't get out of this cot for a couple of weeks at least," she said bitterly. "I took an arrow in the chest. I'll live, but I'll be a while healing."

"Who did it?" he demanded angrily. "The

Wacks?"

"Uhhhh," she hesitated, fearful of what he might do if she told him the truth. If Z was right, and peace was just around the corner, it wouldn't do to have Hickok gun down Tommy and Vint. Well, Vint maybe. But she liked Tommy. "It's all kind of hazy . . ." she finally answered.

"You don't need to talk about it," Hickok told her.

"Thanks."

Hickok shifted, trying to find the right words to say to her. Should he tell her about Bear? What Bear had said? Or let her learn for herself, firsthand, from the horse's mouth, so to speak?

"What are your plans?" she demurely inquired.

"Josh and I are going back to the Home."

"Oh." The single word conveyed her depth of despair.

"Hey! Cheer up!" He tenderly stroked her neck. "I'm coming back."

Bertha averted his gaze. She was confused and emotionally torn by his reserved demeanor.

"I will be back," Hickok vowed. "We're going to the Home to see if the Family will accept the relocation scheme. After the Family votes on it, I'm coming right back. Even if they vote against the plan, I'm coming back. I have a number of things to settle here."

Bertha was at a total loss for words.

"You have some settling to do yourself," he advised her.

"I do?"

"You do."

"I don't understand."

Hickok sighed, weariness pervading his soul.

"What do you mean?" Bertha asked him.

Hickok stared at the tent opening. "I met a friend

of yours. Says the two of you are very . . . close."

"Who?"

"He calls himself Bear."

"Bear?" Bertha leaned forward, delighted. "My good buddy Bear! He's still alive!"

"Yep. He is a . . . friend . . . of yours, then?"

"You bet your white ass!" Bertha giggled. "We went through a lot together. He saved me from Maggot."

"I know."

"Good ol' Bear!" Bertha exclaimed cheerfully. "There wasn't anyone I was closer to when I was with the Porns." She failed to detect the hardening of Hickok's jaw and the narrowing of his blue eyes.

"That's what I gathered," Hickok slowly commented.

"Where is he?" Bertha inquired.

"He's outside." Hickok stood. "I'll tell him you're in here. I don't think he knows."

"No!" she began to protest. "I didn't mean . . ."

"It's okay." He bent over and grabbed the Henry. "I can use the fresh air." He walked to the tent flap.

"Hickok!" Bertha attempted to rise, to follow him, but she was overcome by severe dizziness.

Hickok paused in the tent opening. "Like I told you, I'll be back to see you. While I'm gone, get your affairs straightened out."

"Hickok!"

He was gone, the flap swaying in the breeze.

"Hickok!"

Bertha pushed herself to the edge of the cot and swung her legs over the side. The effort proved too much, and she collapsed onto the pillows, coughing, her right side in agony.

"Hickok," she mumbled, tears filling her eyes, her heart breaking. "Why?"

27

They were walking north on State Highway 47, just the two of them, the afternoon sun beating on them mercilessly.

"The SEAL isn't far," Joshua commented. "I can see the trees up ahead where we hid the transport."

"Yep," Hickok absently nodded.

"You certain you're all right?" Joshua asked.

"How many times do I have to tell you?" Hickok snapped, irritated. "I'm just dandy."

"And rocks can sing."

"What?"

"I realize your personal life is your affair . . ."

"You got that right."

" . . . but I can't help being concerned. You've been moping since I saw you at the Porn head-quarters. If there is anything I can assist you with, dear brother, you know I will."

Hickok stared fondly at Joshua. "Sorry, Josh. I've had a heap on my mind. I've lost a lot on this damn trip, more than I counted on losing."

"I know what you mean," Josh said sadly. "I find

it hard to believe Blade and Geronimo have passed on to the mansions on high."

They reached the field bordering the trees and tramped through the thick grass.

"Me too."

"I wonder if the Wacks got them, or someone else?" Joshua morbidly speculated.

"Does it matter?"

"No. I guess not."

"I just want to get the hell out of here," Hickok said bitterly.

"They didn't want to let us go," Joshua stated, referring to Bear, Zahner, and Reverend Paul. "I think they're worried we might not make it back, despite our good intentions."

"A person never knows when his number is up," Hickok philosophized.

"Let's hear it for optimism!" Joshua grinned.

"I ain't feeling very optimistic these days," Hickok said.

They were almost to the stand of trees.

"Did you hear something?" Hickok stopped and hefted his Henry.

"No." Joshua came to a halt. "Did you?"

"Yep." Hickok moved several steps ahead of Joshua. "Stay behind me. If anything happens, get back to Zahner. I trust him to take care of you."

"But . . ."

Hickok motioned for silence. "Stay here," he whispered.

Joshua nodded.

Hickok crouched and entered the trees, ducking under limbs and carefully circumventing tree trunks and bushes. Had the SEAL been discovered? If so, by whom? The damned Wacks? He doubted anyone could move the vehicle. Blade had locked the doors, and there was no way the impervious body could be breached.

Blade had locked the doors!

Hickok froze, stupefied. How the hell were they going to get inside the vehicle? Blade had the only set of keys! He'd forgotten! His only consolation was that Joshua hadn't realized their predicament either.

The crunch on the twig alerted him to the danger behind him, and he spun, bringing the Henry up, too late.

A powerful figure slammed into him and forced him to the ground, knees gouging his stomach.

Hickok dropped the Henry, his right hand flashing to his Python, the Colt out and up and cocked before he recognized his assailant.

"You crazy Indian!" Hickok exploded. "You almost got yourself killed!"

Geronimo, astride Hickok's chest, reared back and laughed.

"What's so funny?" Hickok demanded.

"You should have seen your face!" Geronimo couldn't contain his hilarity.

"Get off me!" Hickok bellowed. "Only you would pull a stunt like this!"

Geronimo rose to his feet, slapping his thigh in merriment.

"Indians always were sneaking up on the white man," Hickok grumbled as he stood, dusting his buckskins off.

"Admit it." Geronimo grinned. "I got you, but good."

Hickok holstered his Colt, smiled, and clasped his arms around Geronimo. "Damn! It's good to see you, pard!"

There was a crashing in the underbrush behind them, and Joshua broke into view.

"Geronimo!" Joshua shouted. He ran to them and hugged Geronimo, pounding him on the back. "Geronimo! We thought you were dead!"

"And we thought you were dead."

"We?" Hickok questioned hopefully. "Did you say we?"

Geronimo nodded. "He's in the rear of the SEAL. He was pretty beat up when I found him."

Hickok and Joshua rushed to the SEAL and climbed in.

Blade was dozing in the rear section. He roused as they clambered inside, his eyes widening in disbelief. "It can't be!" he said, gaping at his two friends in the back seat.

Hickok glanced at Joshua. "If this is all the welcome we're gonna get, I say we go back into the Twins. Even the Wacks are friendlier than this big lug."

Blade reached for them across the seat, gripping their hands in his. "I thought we lost you," he said, his voice shaking. "I can't believe it!"

"Ever the eloquent sort, eh?" Hickok wisecracked.

"What happened to you?" Joshua asked Blade, pointing at the hole in his pants on his left thigh, the fabric caked with dried blood.

"Arrow," Blade replied. "The Wacks. They came close."

"We all had our share of close calls, pard," Hickok stated.

"We decided to come back here and wait for you," Blade said as Geronimo climbed into the passenger-side bucket seat. "If there was any chance you were still alive, we knew you'd make it back here. We'd about given up hope."

"Where's Bertha?" Geronimo queried.

Hickok glanced at the floor. "She was injured too.

She's with the Nomads, recuperating. She'll be bed-ridden for a couple of weeks. We'll pick her up when we come back.''

"Come back?" Geronimo repeated. "Did I hear you correctly?"

"Sure did, pard," Hickok said.

"Why are we coming back?" Blade inquired. "I don't know about you, but I've had all of this place I can stand."

"Joshua can explain on our way to the Home," Hickok declared.

"What about the equipment Plato wants us to get?" Joshua commented.

"What about it?" Hickok demanded. "The old man doesn't know what we've been through. He'll understand when we come back empty-handed. When we return to the Twins, we'll have all the time we'll need to scour this city for the stuff Plato wants. Another month won't make that much difference, will it?" He turned to Blade.

Blade scratched his head.

"Hickok has a point," Geronimo stressed. "All of us have been battered rather badly. We're not at peak efficiency, and anything less in the Twin Cities can be fatal. I don't see where another month will make any difference." He glanced at Hickok. "Although I'm curious to hear the reason for returning in a month."

"We'll get to that," Hickok said. "How about it, Blade? Do we head for Home, or stay and continue our search for the items Plato wants?"

"All your considerations are valid," Blade stated. "I agree we're not in fighting form, and we can't jeopardize our lives, the SEAL, and our mission by obstinately pursuing our assignment when common sense dictates we should regroup and try again." He grinned at Hickok. "Besides, if we're coming back to the Twin Cities in a month, we can try and get what Plato needs then."

"Then we head for the Home?" Joshua asked.

"We head for the Home." Blade smiled, thinking of Jenny and the reception awaiting him.

"So why are we coming back here in a month?" Geronimo faced Joshua.

"What say we get this show on the road?" Hickok gazed out at the trees. "We can be well out of the Twins by dark."

"Good idea." Blade reached into his right front pocket. "Here." He handed the keys to Hickok.

"You want me to drive?" Hickok took the keys hesitantly.

"I don't think I could, not with my leg the way it is," Blade replied. "And you're the only other one with experience."

Geronimo made a show of rolling his eyes toward the heavens. "Great Spirit! First the Wacks! Then the rats! And now this! Hickok is going to drive again! I must have been overdue for spiritual testing and tribulation!" He smiled at Hickok.

"I see your wonderful, warped sense of humor is still intact, pard," Hickok cracked. He climbed out and back into the SEAL, perching nervously on the driver's seat.

"You can do it, Nathan," Blade said, expressing his confidence in Hickok.

"Piece of cake."

The transport flawlessly turned over, and Hickok carefully backed the vehicle from the trees. He quickly crossed the field and bore north on State Highway 47.

"Back to our Home, sweet Home," Hickok announced as he accelerated.

"I can hardly wait," Blade commented, reclining, placing his hands under the back of his head. "It will be great to see Jenny again."

"I'm relishing the prospect of seeing my parents," Joshua admitted. "I've missed them."

"The trip to the Twin Cities won't be a total loss," Blade stated.

"How do you figure?" Hickok asked, concentrating on his steering, thrilling to the sensation of power and speed conveyed by the SEAL.

"We know what to expect when we return," Blade pointed out. "We won't come blundering into the Twin Cities in the middle of the night again. We won't walk into another trap. We've learned valuable lessons this time. Next time, we'll be prepared."

Hickok chuckled and winked at Joshua.

"What's so funny?" Blade inquired.

"Nothing," Hickok smirked.

"I know you better than that," Blade said thoughtfully. "What is so funny about the prospect of coming back here?"

"Speaking of coming back," Geronimo chipped in, "isn't it about time for Joshua to tell us why we need to come back to the Twin Cities in a month?"

"Yep. Tell him, Josh," Hickok urged.

So Joshua did, meticulously narrating his stay with the Horns, his mission to the Porns, and the resultant summit meeting of the leaders of the three factions.

"Incredible," Blade commented after Joshua finished.

"You are a very special man," Geronimo said to Joshua.

"Me? I didn't do anything unusual," Joshua disagreed.

"You most definitely did," Blade corrected him. "Surely you realize what you might have achieved? You might be the one responsible for bringing about peace between groups who have been warring for years and years. That's quite an accomplishment."

"Ideally, all men and women should live in peace with one another," Joshua stated, glancing at Hickok, "although I am now willing to concede that occasionally circumstances arise compelling a person to violent action."

Hickok looked at Joshua in the rearview mirror. "About time you came around to my way of thinking." He grinned.

"Any peace between the three factions," Joshua said to Blade, "is predicated on the Family's reception of the relocation idea."

"I'm positive we'll come up with something," Blade stated confidently. "Plato will want to help. You can count on that."

"I know." Joshua nodded slowly, then sighed. "I do have one regret, however."

"What's that?" Geronimo inquired.

"I wasn't able to persuade the others to include the Wacks in the peace initiative. Surely the Wacks crave peace as much as the rest. It was unfair to exclude them."

Geronimo gazed at Blade. "You better tell him."

"Tell me what?" Joshua twisted in the back seat so he could face Blade.

"I was a guest of the Wacks for a while," Blade began. "I don't recommend them as hosts."

"What happened?" Joshua wanted to know.

For the next twenty minutes, Blade told them of his experiences with the Wacks. He detailed his capture, the staking out, the incident with the nightmarish Fant, and his escape.

"It must have been horrible," Joshua said when Blade paused.

"Ahhh," Blade added. "I've neglected to mention the best part. But it isn't really my story. It's

Geronimo's."

"After Blade and I hooked up," Geronimo said, immediately taking up the account, "we hid for twelve hours in a ruined house. Several times the Wacks came close, searching for Blade, but they didn't find us. Blade wanted me to sneak back to their base of operations, that Hospital for the Criminally Insane, and try and spot his Commando or the Vega automatics. So, as the sun was setting, I worked my way to a building near the hospital. I climbed to the second floor and observed the Wacks from a window." He paused, frowning at the memory.

"What did you see?" Joshua anxiously asked.

"I didn't see the Fant thing," Geronimo responded. "Although I wish I had! Can you imagine! Anyway, I didn't spot the guns. None of the Wacks were carrying firearms."

"You avoided my question," Joshua remarked.

"No. I'm getting to that." Geronimo closed his eyes. "The creature had killed a number of Wacks by crushing them to death. I stood in that window and watched several dozen Wacks eat their fallen comrades."

"Eat?" Hickok chimed in. "Then it's true, the reports about the Wacks being cannibals?"

"Yes, it's true," Geronimo shuddered. "The Wacks were clustered around the bodies, or what was left of them. They would dip their hands into the . . . mess . . . and stuff their mouths. I can't imagine a more grisly sight than the one I witnessed."

"Dear Father!" Joshua exclaimed.

"Something will need to be done about the Wacks," Blade commented. He stared out at the passing scenery. "I can't wait to get back to the Home," he reiterated. "Just can't wait."

"I'm looking forward to it myself, pard," Hickok said.

"Any special reason?" Geronimo idly inquired.

"Yep." Hickok glanced down, his nose crinkling.

"Want to tell us about it?" Geronimo asked.

"I've never needed a new set of buckskins so badly in my whole life."

"They look like you washed them recently," Geronimo noted.

"I did."

"He had to," Joshua mentioned.

"Had to?" Geronimo eyed Hickok quizzically.

"Let's just say I've learned a very valuable lesson," Hickok said. "A new appreciation for nature."

"I don't get it," Geronimo admitted.

"I'm never, ever, gonna pee on a tree again."

"Oh?"

"Hey, Blade!" Hickok called back, adroitly changing the subject. "How are you holding up?"

"Just fine," Blade answered sleepily. "Be sure and watch out for the bumps. I'm going to get some sleep, if you aren't having any problems handling the SEAL."

"Like I told you before, it's a piece of cake."

Make the Most of Your
Leisure Time
with
LEISURE BOOKS

Please send me the following titles:

Quantity	Book Number	Price
_____	_____	_____
_____	_____	_____
_____	_____	_____
_____	_____	_____
_____	_____	_____

If out of stock on any of the above titles, please send me the alternate title(s) listed below:

_____	_____	_____
_____	_____	_____
_____	_____	_____
_____	_____	_____

Postage & Handling _____

Total Enclosed $_____

☐ Please send me a free catalog.

NAME _____
(please print)

ADDRESS _____

CITY _____ STATE _____ ZIP _____

Please include $1.00 shipping and handling for the first book ordered and 25¢ for each book thereafter in the same order. All orders are shipped within approximately 4 weeks via postal service book rate. PAYMENT MUST ACCOMPANY ALL ORDERS.*

*Canadian orders must be paid in US dollars payable through a New York banking facility.

Mail coupon to: **Dorchester Publishing Co., Inc.
6 East 39 Street, Suite 900
New York, NY 10016
Att: ORDER DEPT.**